# Talking With The Dead

*An FBI Psychics Prequal*

Shiloh Walker

ISBN: 9781090317988

# DEDICATION

It's March 2019 as I get this book ready for print.
Two years since I realized I was looking at losing one of my brothers.

Looking back, I should have realized we'd been moving down this road for much, much longer. The guilt of not seeing it is something that eats at me, even though I know all about the hindsight and twenty/twenty thing.

I just wished I'd seen it sooner, how much pain you were in. But the time I did…you were slipping so far away, I didn't know how to reach you and every time I looked at you, every time I saw you or spoke to you, the pain you carried, the shadows…it was all getting worse.

Some part of me tried to pretend I didn't know what was coming, but I did. I still tried to save you and I did things that I know made you hate me for a while.

At the end, I hope you know I fought for you because I loved you, that I still do. I always will. I hope you forgave me.

I know you just wanted peace and I'm not angry with you. Whatever anger I had inside, I let go of a long time ago.

But dear God…I miss you.

You better be working on the mural for us in Heaven, too.

# PROLOGUE

Although Lucas never mentioned it, and neither did Mom, Michael O'Rourke was a disappointment and he knew it.

Lucas, now, Lucas was everything their charlatan mother could ever hope for. She'd taught him well, teaching him how to run scams, how to pick pockets and how to evade cops and social workers. Yeah, she'd taught him well, all right—maybe too well. Lucas was sixteen. Strong. Smart. He wasn't going to hang around and keep helping his mother run her scams.

She called herself Lavonne, but her birth name was Rachel O'Rourke. Her great gift in life was in the grift. She could run a scam like nothing Michael had ever seen. Even Lucas couldn't sucker them in the way Mama could.

But Lucas had gifts, *real* gifts, the kind Mama liked to pretend she had. He saw things.

The "sight" Mama called it. Ran in her family, she liked to say, although Michael didn't think she had ever seen anything that he couldn't see with his own two eyes. Lucas once told Mike that their mama couldn't see a spirit if it bit her on the ass. They'd laughed themselves sick, thinking about it.

Lucas could see, though. He *knew* things. He had known when it was time to leave New Orleans and he had known when it was time to leave Memphis and he had warned her about going to Nashville. She'd pissed people off there, but Lavonne was stupid. Plain and simple. She was going to do what she wanted to do.

She got herself embroiled in shit and then slid away before it was time to pay the piper. Her luck wouldn't last forever. Lucas just hoped it would hold a little while longer. He was going to get the hell away from her. One night, while she was screwing some dude for drug money, Lucas and Mike were going to disappear. It was going to have to be soon. Mike wasn't safe around Lavonne. Last night, Lucas had overheard Lavonne talking to a major freak—she'd offered the guy an hour alone with Mike for a grand. Of course, the man wanted to see Mike first. Too bad, too. The guy was mean enough, if he had paid Lavonne upfront and then they couldn't find Mike, he might have killed her.

Lucas wanted her dead. More than anything, he wanted their mother dead. That had been the eighth time he had saved Mike from being raped. Mike knew about that one—he'd been with Lucas when Lavonne was trying to pimp the twelve year old out. He had been there three other times, too. But he knew nothing about all the other times and Lucas planned on keeping it that way.

They had to get out of there. Sooner or later, Lavonne would try to set it up when Lucas wasn't around.

Lucas was pissed off. He'd been mad ever since last night and Mike knew why. His gut had been twisted into slimy, sick knots all night but today, he wasn't so worried about it. Lucas had gotten him away. Lucas had protected him. Again. Lucas was always there—even though he was smart enough, looked old enough, he could get away from Lavonne whenever he wanted. He didn't though.

Mike knew why.

No, he didn't have any special sight and he couldn't see inside a person's mind. But he did have a bond, a close one, with his big brother. They could talk. Carry on entire conversations all without even moving their lips.

*"She's been drinking again,"* Michael said. He didn't have to tell Lucas that. The older boy would have seen it long before Michael did. Still, being able to talk this way with Lucas made him feel special. Lucas made him feel special. Lucas made him feel wanted.

Didn't make him feel like he was some useless baby that he had to lug around, or worse—like some worthless piece of crap that shouldn't have ever been born.

*"Gee—ya think?"* Lucas said. Even his mental voice had a sardonic tone to it and the smile on his mouth was a bitter one. His blue eyes met Michael's in the mirror for the briefest of seconds before he went back to pretending to focus on the book in his hands.

Lucas loved reading. Neither of them had ever spent any serious time in school unless a social worker arrived on the scene. Then their mother would pretend to get all weepy, begging for forgiveness and understanding. No matter how times it happened, Lavonne managed to convince the effing government that she was ready to change. She'd do it this time. She loved her babies and just couldn't make it without them. She really would get sober and straight and blah blah blah. Mike knew all that garbage by heart, just like he knew every last bit of it was a lie.

She might love Lucas but that was because he was her meal ticket. But she didn't give a damn about Mike. Anybody with eyes should have seen it, Mike figured. But he was tired of hoping that they would take him away. She suckered them all. They'd go to whatever school was close by for a few days and then they'd disappear, moving on to another city where the process would start all over again. Two years ago, their mother had finally gotten smart.

If she moved around enough, no social worker could keep track of her.

So they rarely stopped moving. Since then, Michael and Lucas hadn't slept in the same place for more than a week. It sucked, but it was better than dealing with the shit they had to put up with when their mother went all ballistic the second the social worker left.

But school or no, Lucas loved to read and he had passed that passion onto his kid brother. As long as Michael kept his books hidden from her, of course. She liked to take them away and burn them, right in front of him. He learned pretty damn quick that he had to hide them from her. Lucas, though, he didn't have to worry about that. Lucas didn't have to dodge her fists, he didn't ever go hungry, and he could read as much as he wanted, as long as he got his work done.

Michael didn't mind. It wasn't like it was Lucas' fault that Lavonne loved Lucas, but hated Michael. It wasn't like her love was some big prize. Her love was almost as revolting as her hate—Mike had seen the way she liked to cuddle up to Lucas, petting him like he was some teddy bear. The bigger and older Lucas got, the more attentive she became. She looked at him with greed in her eyes and Mike knew what that look meant. So did Lucas.

Mike sighed and rested his head against the window. She'd dragged them out of bed before sunrise this time and he was worn out. He wanted to sleep, but he didn't dare sleep if she was driving. Later, she'd get in the back seat and get stoned. Once she passed out and Lucas was driving, Mike would feel safe enough to sleep. The streetlights sped by in a blur and Mike glanced toward the front seat. She was edging up over ninety as she weaved in and out of traffic.

*"She don't slow down, we'll get pulled over."*

Michael felt Lucas' mental laughter, the kind that wasn't really laughing at anything. *"We should be so lucky."* But Lucas looked up, and from the rearview mirror, Mike saw the thoughtful way his eyes narrowed, saw the distant, off focus look form there. "Lavonne, I think you might want to slow down," Lucas said levelly.

They couldn't call her Mama. Or Mom. Nothing like that. She didn't like it. She blew out some smoke before drawing once more on the cigarette in her mouth, her voice low and rough from years of smoking. "Why would I want to do that?" she rasped.

"Cops," Lucas replied, shrugging one shoulder.

She scowled and slammed on the brake so hard that Michael went flying into the seat in front of them and the car behind them laid on the horn for a good thirty seconds. Mike glanced over his shoulder as he eased back onto the seat. The driver of the black sedan flipped them off.

"What in the hell are you looking back there for?" Lavonne snapped. "Bastard was tailgating me. Ain't my fault."

"Yes, Lavonne," he said automatically. She sent him a dirty look. Michael could see the hatred in her eyes. Then it was gone and she looked at Lucas, her expression irritated. "Damn it. You feel cops around and you're just now telling me?"

She hated him. She always had. She always would.

But Michael didn't care. He had Lucas. That was all that mattered. He stared out the window, eyes searching for patrol cars. He saw nothing.

But if Lucas said there was cops, then there was cops.

Funny, though, how Michael had thought it…and then Lucas mentioned it.

ଓଃ

"You can't take my boy!"

Michael hid in the attic, huddled in a tight little ball, frozen with shock and fear. He stared through the tiny crack, watching as the big guy busted Lucas in the mouth again.

*Help him.* He had to go help Lucas. They were going to kill him.

Whatever Lavonne had done this time, she had done it to the wrong people and they were going to kill Lucas because of it.

*No. I can't let them.* He started to get up, for probably the fifth time. And just like the past four times, Lucas did something to him. Michael felt his muscles freeze, felt his body shut down. His arms and legs refused to obey him, following the silent commands from his brother as Michael sank back into his hiding place.

"Now didn't I tell you not to come back here without my money, Rachel?" It was a big, mean looking guy. Mike had seen him before. His head was bald on top, long on the sides and back. He always wore it slicked back in a ponytail and he spoke with an accent like the guys in that movie, *The Godfather.*

Her eyes were red with tears but she forced a smile at him. "That's why I came back, baby. I got some money and I got a line in to get more."

"Yeah. I bet you do. You think you can find enough johns to cover the 5k?" He curled his lip and gave Lavonne a very long slow once-over. "Not with that used up snatch."

Her face turned an ugly red, but she didn't say anything other than, "I got a plan, Mitch. Promise."

Mitch just laughed. "Sure." He looked around the small space and demanded, "Where's the brat?"

"Leave Lucas alone and I'll tell you," Lavonne said, crying.

Michael flinched. If Lavonne knew where to find him, then she *would* trade him for Lucas. Not that Michael wouldn't do the same—he'd walked through fire for Lucas, sell his soul to the devil for him.

Pretty damn clear that was what the old lady wanted to do. Even though she'd tried to do it before, hearing it all over again really sucked.

"You fucking bitch," Lucas seethed. Hatred blazed in Lucas' eyes and he snarled at Lavonne. He struggled against the men holding him, determined to get his hands on his mother. "I'd rather die now then let them get their hands on my brother."

Lavonne ignored him, moving to one of the men in the apartment, stroking her hands down his arm as she whispered, "Mikey's young. You're bound to know somebody who'd like a boy like him. People that would pay five grand, easy. More. Just leave Lucas…I need him—"

"*Bitch!*" Lucas roared, trying to break free of the two men holding him.

Michael's belly pitched and rolled from all the emotions he felt flooding off of Lucas, and through Lucas, he felt the emotions of the others. Hatred, greed, boredom… He buried his face in his hands, wishing he could just disappear. For good. Forever.

"He's just a worthless brat. Not like you, baby," Lavonne said, forcing a shaking smile at her son before looking back at the guy who looked like he was in charge. "So what do you say? You can get some good money. A trade, the kid for whatever I owed you."

The man laughed as he backhanded Lavonne with casual ease. "No. I'd rather take the one you want the most," he responded. Standing aside, he jerked his head toward the door.

From the attic, Michael watched in horror as they dragged his brother away.

It seemed like hours passed as Michael lay frozen in shock. He couldn't move until the old lady was gone. If he did, she was going to take this out on him. And Michael knew he wouldn't survive the beating this time around. Lucas wasn't there to save him.

Lucas…

Oh, God. Raw pain ripped through him, followed by terror, guilt and too many other emotions for him to understand. Lucas might never be there again. The way that guy had looked at Lavonne as his boys dragged Lucas away—he had *smiled.* Lavonne screamed.

He was going to…to… *No. You can't think like that. Get moving. Save him.*

But he couldn't get moving. Not until Lavonne was gone. It didn't take long, though. She screamed and cried for a few minutes after they dragged Lucas away, but in typical Lavonne fashion, she was more interested in saving her ass than anybody else's. Even Lucas'.

She packed in a hurry, throwing her stuff into a sack and leaving behind everything else. When she walked out, she had a bag full of clothes in one hand, a bottle of whiskey in the other and she never once looked back.

Now that she was finally gone, he could sneak down and take the money Lucas had been hoarding, get some food—then Michael was going to find his brother and they were going to get the hell out of there, as far away from Lavonne and her crap as they could.

Michael wasn't thinking of her as Mama any more. Not Mom.

Not anything. She was no relation to him.

She was no blood. She was no family.

She was scum, less than that. The shit she had got herself into was why Lucas was in trouble. The man had come looking for money she owed him and Lucas was the one paying the price. She'd been willing to give away her own son to pay off her trouble.

Gingerly, he climbed down from the attic, still listening, well aware she might be waiting out in the hall to see if he came out. But he figured she was probably long gone. The bastards who took Lucas may decide to come back and she wouldn't want to be anywhere close, just in case.

She sure as hell hadn't been concerned about leaving him behind, had she?

No. "Not my blood, not any more," he whispered furiously, working open the tiny slit in the mattress he and Lucas shared. There was money there. A lot of it. More than Lavonne could even imagine having her hands on. Lucas was careful, and he was smart.

They were going to be okay. Unaware of the tears that rolled down his cheeks, Michael jerked out the little bag that held the money, tucking it inside the waistband of his shorts and using duct tape to make sure it stayed in place. They would be just fine.

He crept out the window in the bedroom after he grabbed a pack of crackers, some peanut butter and the stash of candy bars Lucas had hidden from Lavonne. It wasn't much food but it would have to do. Michael had to get out of there.

His young, twelve-year-old mind never questioned the urgency that filled him. He just knew he had to *go*.

Night had fallen and he stayed in the shadows as he moved out of the alley. Had to stay away from everybody. Both the dealers on the streets and the cops who cruised through the streets of Nashville. Had to get out. Get away.

But Lucas first.

The bond between them hadn't ever been closed off before. Michael needed to be able to feel Lucas to find him. But it was like Lucas was hiding from him.

Finally he was able to reach out and touch his brother's mind and he could have cried with relief. Huddled in the back of the old garage, he rubbed at his gritty eyes and called out to Lucas.

But Lucas shoved him back. *"Get away, Mikey. Now."*

Although he didn't know the reason, Michael heard the panic in

Lucas' voice, panic and a fear he hadn't ever heard from Lucas before. *"Where are you? We got to get out of here."*

*"You go, Mikey. Go now—"*

The scream that tore through Lucas echoed from Michael as well. And suddenly, Michael wasn't in the old garage any more. He was in a cold room with gray walls and he *hurt.*

Terror flooded Michael and he flinched as Lucas' voice filled his head and sounded off the walls in the room. *"Mikey, go!"*

The people who surrounded them stared all around, looking at each other before looking back at Michael…no, Lucas. They were looking at Lucas. Michael was just feeling the same damn things, seeing the same things as Lucas.

The hot metallic taste of fear filled his mouth and he tried to break away, but he couldn't.

*"Mikey…"*

There was a gun pointing at him.

*"Lucas!"*

*"I'm sorry, Mikey. We were going to…"*

The horrendous crack filled the air, and then there was darkness.

Michael came screaming out of the darkness, struggling against the arms that held him. But he was alone.

Alone in the garage.

And Lucas was gone. Dead.

# CHAPTER ONE

The scent of blood, gore and earth wasn't a scent that a man forgot easily. Gun drawn, Special Agent Michael O'Rourke breathed through his mouth and tried not to pay attention to the smell. It was hard, but he had done this often enough that he could block it out a little.

A few of the less experienced agents were feeling pretty squeamish. That was more a distraction than the smell—at least for Mike. Their nausea hit him like a sucker punch, right in the gut, and he had to battle back the same bile that they were fighting to contain.

None of them had the luxury to get sick right now. Samuel Watkins had killed six times and his seventh victim was running out of time. Michael could feel her, too. He could feel her terror, her pain. She wanted her mama, but she didn't dare cry out. Brave little thing.

*I'll get you to your mama, sweetheart. I promise.* Not one more child would die because of this bastard.

It was darker than midnight down there and descending the steps was like a descent straight into hell. Dark, ugly, and terrifying. Mike wasn't afraid of Watkins. The worst thing Watkins could do to him was kill him and Mike would go happily if it meant taking the monster with him. No. He was afraid that Watkins would find the girl and finish what he had started.

But Watkins was preoccupied. As Mike reached the bottom of

the stairs, his booted feet hit the dirt floor and he went still, staring at the sight before him. Faint greenish lights hovered around Watkins and the short, stout man was flailing at the air with fisted hands. He was also screaming.

"What the…"

Destin Mortin came to a dead stop just at Mike's shoulder. A new agent in Oz's little motley crew, Destin couldn't see ghosts. Her skill was a little odd, even to Mike. She fit in well, though, on this case. Officially, Destin was still in training. Unofficially, she was ready to take to the streets and kick some ass. Oz was worried that Destin would get to Watkins first and take out several pounds of flesh. That morning, Mike would have agreed with Oz. It was completely possible that Destin might find Watkins first and seek some good old-fashioned vigilante justice.

Wasn't going to happen though.

Samuel Watkins wasn't going to leave this basement alive.

He was already a little gray in the face, although it was hard to really judge his color well with the ghostly lights flashing around him. As one of the spirits moved closer, it solidified and a girl's face became visible. Mike recognized her from the missing person's file. Misty Brighton had disappeared on her tenth birthday. She had been Watkins' first victim. She'd been dead for eight years.

She looked toward him. A mean little smile curled her lips and Mike said softly, "It's time, Misty. You can go on now."

Misty shook her head. *"Not yet."* Her voice was wispy and insubstantial, but it had an underscore of rage. It burned with a blistering intensity that stung Mike's skin. She reached out and Mike winced as she stuck a ghostly hand inside Watkins' chest. The man screamed. It was a high-pitched, terrified sound. It ended abruptly and then Watkins collapsed, falling forward.

Mike stood there, staring at the man who had raped and murdered six girls. He lay face down in the dirt, still as death.

Misty lifted her head and Mike waited, apprehension drawing his skin tight. Would she go? Or would the rage bind her here?

"Your mom is waiting for you," he said gently.

Misty's eyes closed and her form became more and more insubstantial. *"I'm scared, Michael."*

He smiled at her. "I know. But there's nothing to be afraid of, not now. Not any more."

At least, not for her.

ଔଓ

Death did ugly things to a person.

Tanya had been so pretty. The body on the ground couldn't possibly be one of Daisy's friends. It just wasn't possible. Death had turned her pretty, sweet face into a macabre mask and her toned body had long since gone through rigor, her limbs limp and flaccid.

Just like the others, she'd been raped, beat, strangled. But she'd bled out. That was what had killed her. There was no pooling of fluids, no mottling. The coroner would find very little, if any, blood left in Tanya's corpse. So far, Daisy had counted more than twenty shallow little slices. It would have been very, very slow.

"Ten minutes."

Daisy looked over her shoulder at Deputy Wyatt Lock. Lock was staring at Tanya with a mixture of grief, horror and disbelief. "Wyatt?"

He turned his head and met Daisy's gaze. His normally mild hazel eyes were burning with fury and his voice throbbed with intensity as he said, "I want ten minutes alone with him, Daisy."

*Get in line.* When she managed to get her hands on the killer, if she didn't kill him herself, she was going to have her hands full keeping him safe while he awaited trial. The thought of a trial made Daisy get her ass in gear. They had a crime scene to secure and there couldn't be a single mistake. Everything had to be done perfect and legal, because this bastard wasn't going to get off due to a lack of evidence or some damned legal loophole.

He was going to pay for what he was doing and he was going to pay dearly.

She stepped aside and beckoned for the crime scene photographer to get to work. It was a grim and thankless task and by the time it was over, Daisy was hovering between wanting to scream bloody murder and breaking down into tears. She would have settled for a nice, stiff drink but she wasn't going to get that either.

A man was standing at the very edge of the crime scene and

only the four volunteer firefighters were keeping him from running up to Tanya's body. "Hurry it up," she said in a low voice as she passed Wyatt. "He can't see her like that."

Daisy approached Tom Dourant and said the words that every cop hated.

ଔ

It took two more days to finish up the paperwork. By the time he had fulfilled that particular pain in the ass obligation, he was ready to leave Philadelphia behind and never, ever return.

Whether or not that would happen, Mike had no idea.

He left a message on Oz's machine and told her that he'd be out of contact for a while and then he turned off his pager. If she needed him badly enough, she'd find him anyway.

But he had to get away. Had to clear his head and hopefully get away from the ghosts that chased him. He doubted it would work, but he was going to give it a shot. There were other problems in Philly, but somebody else was going to have to handle them.

Destin had to stay in the City of Brotherly Love and she had a decent partner in Caleb Durand. Those two could handle the bad vibes that were keeping the agents awake at night, and they could do it without Mike's help. His grip on sanity often seemed pretty slippery, but never as much as it did now.

If he didn't get away and get a break, they might as well lock him up now and throw the keys in the Delaware. He wouldn't be good for anything else. He didn't bother checking out of the hotel. The Bureau would handle his tab. They also would have paid for the cab he called, but since he didn't want them tracking his every step, he paid the driver in cash.

The driver left him in the drop off zone without a thank you for the five dollar tip. Mike hoped the guy would go and buy some deodorant and an air freshener. The guy reeked to high heaven. He could still smell the oily stink of unwashed body ten minutes later as he waited in line for a rental car.

It meant using a credit card and ID, but he would have to show ID to get a flight out of the city anyway. Losing one's self was a lot harder since 9/11. Normally, Mike wouldn't care. Normally, he was of the mind that there wasn't enough being done to make the country secure. But this one time, he really, really wished he could just disappear and nobody be able to find him.

Michael's appetite for food was dead.

He'd come in here, starving. After nothing but fast food for the past couple months, a decent home cooked meal sounded like heaven. But five seconds after sitting down, all thoughts of food had fled his mind. He sat staring at the Formica table top while dread, anger and disgust formed a leaden ball in the pit of his belly.

*Am I ever going to get a break?* he wondered bleakly. There was no answer and he didn't really expect one.

Too tired for this mess, he almost climbed off the chair and walked back to his car. He could put the top down on the powerful little convertible, hit the gas and be miles away before dark. He could put two or three states between himself and this darkness, and just maybe, he could forget about it.

But even though he was tired and dancing on the edge of depression, he couldn't make himself leave. The darkness in the air was too thick, and the violence too recent. It sat on the back of his tongue like something gone sour. He lowered his shields and opened himself up to the darkness hovering.

It was more than just darkness though. It was something bloody. Something evil.

This small town in Indiana was quiet, damn it. He had found the little bitty dot on the map at the rest area right inside the state's border and figured it was as good a place as any to get some rest. A good a place as any to get away from the darkness, the death.

The ghosts.

As always, Mike had been wrong. In a major way. The ghosts were here, just like they had been everywhere he had gone for the past two decades. They followed him. Why in the hell he'd thought he could get away from them here, now, he'd never know. These ghosts were his only companions in life and for as long as he lived, they'd find him.

After twenty years, he was even used to it. The company of ghosts was a sight better than being left alone with his thoughts. But he didn't like the darkness he felt here. Not at all. He didn't even have to ask around to know that something very, very bad was going on.

Something bad seemed to be his reason for existing. Like a moth drawn to flame, he was drawn unconsciously to places just like this, places where an evil lived, an evil that he would have to hunt down. He hadn't felt any inkling of wrong as he drove here. Nothing as he entered the small town. Mike had actually thought, finally, for once, he had gotten away from them at least for a while.

It wasn't that he thought he could leave them behind forever, although he sure as hell wouldn't mind it. But after the last job, he needed some peace. Some silence. Just a little bit of time to pretend that he was normal.

Mike hadn't ever been normal, even before he picked up his bizarre little talent. When it first came on him, he had run away from it. Half out of his mind from fear and slowly going insane as he tried to get away from the people that few others saw.

The counselor who had finally helped him to understand what was going on was gone now. Michael had been close to sixteen before he made sense of the things and voices and sights crowding his mind. Even Lucas had no idea what had been done to him that night when Michael had shared in his brother's death.

Elizabeth Ransome had looked at the child lying in the hospital bed and she had understood. She saw a boy who was nearly a man, one who was terrified and tormented, but not insane. More, she helped Michael understand.

She saw somebody with a gift. A terrible, unpleasant gift, but a gift nonetheless. *You can let this gift rule you and drive you crazy, or you can learn to use it. Save others from dying like your brother did, Michael. Let me help you. Then we can help them.*

She had helped him make sense of the people he saw that others couldn't see, the voices he heard that nobody else could hear.

Yeah, if Elizabeth hadn't come along, he would have gone insane. Sooner or later, he'd have even managed to succeed when he attempted suicide.

He knew that.

It was getting to him again, though. He was losing his distance, losing his focus. Mike was walking too damned close to the brink again, too much death, too many voices that had been silenced long before their time. Michael had to learn how to block them out again.

This last case had damned near destroyed him.

Baby killer.

That was what Samuel Watkins had been. He hadn't died a painful enough death. His heart had stopped. The official report was heart attack, but unofficially, he had been scared to death by one of his first victims. Too damned easy—he had taken six young lives. Six sweet, innocent young lives in a way so brutal, so horrifying and perverted that it had taken everything Mike had just to stay on the case.

Those little faces haunted him at night. Not their ghosts—no, they had passed on once their killer saw justice. Even Misty had finally let go, leaving this earth to go on to what waited beyond.

But the knowledge that he hadn't been quick enough to save them filled him with bitter, tired anger. Six lives lost, forever gone. Their leaving had left gaping, raw wounds in the lives of their parents and siblings. And inside of Michael. Although he didn't know them until after they had died, he felt their absence acutely.

Too late. He was always too late. This was the story of his life. He came in after the horrors happened and tried to piece things back together again.

It was destroying him.

The tiny chiming of a bell over the door intruded on his brooding and he glanced up automatically before returning his attention to the plate in front of him. It held no appeal for him, but he knew if he didn't eat, he'd never rebuild the strength he had drained tracking down Watkins.

Energy crackled through the room as a cool breeze from the outdoors came gusting through the door just before it closed. Like static electricity, the energy danced down his skin, shocking him, sizzling under his flesh, bursting through his mind like fireworks on the Fourth of July.

Slowly, he raised his eyes from the unappetizing food and found himself staring at a snug little backside covered in khaki as a woman boosted herself onto a stool at the café counter. Her hair was golden brown, caught in a thick braid that hung more than halfway down her back. As he watched her shrug out of the rather official looking jacket, Michael cursed the blood that was suddenly running hot through his veins.

This was a distraction that he didn't want and didn't need.

First the dark cloud that had taken hold of his mind and now all he could smell was the faint tropical fragrance that drifted from the woman's hair and the soft vanilla of her skin.

And the purpose that filled her entire being. It was like she was walking around wrapped with neon, but only Mike could see it.

Anger.

Frustration.

Rage.

*Bingo.* The woman was all but a walking, talking cry for help and Mike just didn't know if he could take any more on right now. Then he blew out a breath and muttered, "You can handle it. You always do."

Rolling his eyes skyward, he thought silently, *But it would be so nice to actually be able to have a relaxing vacation.*

A soft, familiar voice echoed in his mind, *"Then maybe you should try some remote cabin in Alaska. Might be a few less unsolved murders out in the middle of nowhere."*

Years of practice had taught him not to flinch, not to jump, not to even look directly at the man speaking to him. Nobody else would see him. He had been dead for twenty years. *"How's the afterlife, Lucas?"* he asked dryly, arching a brow as he nonchalantly turned his gaze to stare at his brother.

*"Ever the smart ass, Mikey."* A slow smile tugged up Lucas' lips in a grin that haunted Michael's sleep. *"You know, you could move into one of those glacier caves. I bet not too many people have been murdered in one of those. You can get some peace there."*

Lucas' face was forever young. Some movies painted ghosts as grisly images, but it had been Michael's experience that a ghost was an echo of what the ghost remembered seeing in life. Lucas looked exactly as he had the last time he'd seen himself, standing in the bathroom, running his hands through his hair. Wavy brown hair, a little too long, blue eyes surrounded by spiky lashes that both of the brothers had inherited—and hated. Thin to the point of being bony, with big hands, big shoulders. Exactly as Michael had looked at that age. Mike had grown into his body—Lucas hadn't been given the chance.

Forever young. Forever handsome.

*"You're becoming pretty damned moody, Mikey."*

A tiny smile lit his face. Nobody but Lucas had ever called him Mikey. And even though he had most likely passed the age where Mikey was an acceptable name, hearing it from Lucas was oddly comforting. Just like seeing him was comforting. But at the same time, Mike hated seeing him.

He interacted with ghosts on a regular basis and they only hung around the living for as long as they had. Once their business was finished, they passed on.

Lucas had been waiting for twenty years to finish his business and he didn't seem to be in any hurry to move on now, either.

*"When are you going to move on, Luc?"*

*"When I make sure I keep a promise. Promise is a promise, Mike. I told you I'd make sure you were happy. That's when I'll move on."*

With a sigh, Michael shoved a hand through his hair. This was an old conversation, one they'd had a hundred times. *"There is something wrong here."*

Lucas lifted one shoulder in a restless shrug. *"I know. I felt it this morning. Young people. A lot of blood. Some old. Some fresh. But something is definitely not right in Smalltown America."*

Michael suspected the lady sitting on the stool in front of him had answers. He could see it in her weary, bitter eyes and the way she sat. Although she sat tall and straight with her shoulders pulled back, there was an invisible weight bearing down on her.

He didn't need to see the shiny brass badge on her jacket to know what he was looking at.

Cop.

From under the fringe of his lashes, he sat back and studied her. It was there in the purposefulness of her walk, the way she held herself, in the tense frustration he felt rolling off of her. *"Go ask her,"* Lucas suggested.

*"Stranger in town, asking if there's something odd going on in her town. Oh, yes, excellent way to not attract attention."* Michael shot that idea down as he shoved the sandwich on his plate around.

*"If you don't eat that, you're going to be sorry later."*

Michael curled up his lip and slowly lifted the sandwich, trying to tune his brother out as he bit into the pile of meat, cheese and bread. It had about as much flavor and appeal as a sawdust sandwich would, but he knew he needed it.

*"That's a good boy,"* Lucas teased, reaching out to pat Michael's head.

Michael felt the touch like a cool wind on his scalp. It didn't bother him anymore when the dead touched him. But he still slid Lucas a look and silently said, *"Fuck off, man."*

Lucas might be dead, but he was still Michael's brother.

ଓଃଠ

Dasynda Crandall saw the guy sitting at the far end of counter and summed him up with a fairly quick glance as she crossed the café. Built, handsome, and something about the look in his eyes added *not to be messed with* to her list.

He made her back itch, but she couldn't exactly say she felt something off about him. Not that she could really trust her instincts much any more. Her first guess would be that this was a decent guy for the most part, even if he did look a little too big and a little too scary to set the mind at ease.

But Daisy's instincts just plain sucked, as far as she was concerned. She had a damned killer in her town and she wasn't getting so much as an inkling on who it was.

Her instincts had always served her well, but they had four bodies now, and no clue about the killer. Daisy was frustrated beyond all belief. Why in the hell had murders started *after* she had taken office?

This was why she had left the Louisville Metro Police Department. The instincts she had lived her life by seemed to be failing her. Women she had known all her life were being killed and Daisy didn't even know where to start.

She watched the stranger from the mirror that had hung over Elsa's cash register for a good twenty years. Even though Elsa had finally given up the fifties and the beehive hairdo, she still kept that mirror and checked her cardinal red coiffure rather regularly. Daisy watched as the man glanced to his right on a regular basis. Like he would if he was talking to somebody.

But his lips never moved. And there was nobody there. The food on his plate didn't seem to interest him much, but she did see him finally eat some of it. He had some of Elsa's world famous pot roast on that sandwich, but he might as well have been chewing bark for all the enjoyment he showed as he took yet another bite.

Forcing her attention back to her own food, she started to eat. To think. She didn't want to think about the killer. Thinking about it reminded her just how incompetent she had become. But she hadn't ever been one to run from her problems and she sure as hell couldn't run from this one.

There had to be something somewhere. No killer could come and go without a trace like this.

But what in the hell was going on in her town?

The image of Tanya's body danced before her eyes and her stomach pitched. Tanya hadn't just been killed. She had been tortured. Raped repeatedly. Strangled so brutally it had damned near crushed her throat. When death had finally come, it had come slowly, her blood trickling out so she was aware of exactly what was coming. Her death had been slow and horrific.

Daisy's fondest wish in life was to mete out that same brutal death to the man who had killed Tanya. Dropping the sandwich, she shoved the plate away and propped her arms on the counter.

"I'm going to find you," she whispered harshly. "Just wait."

# CHAPTER TWO

Somebody was having fantasies at that moment.

Oh, he was going to have fun with her. The young ones were always the best. She didn't know him—he would miss out on that initial shock, the denial, when they came swimming up out of sleep and saw him for the first time. He did enjoy seeing that look on their face. Enjoyed listening to them beg and plead…*why are you doing this to me?* Then they'd try to bargain. *I have kids—babies. They need me. You know they need me.*

Yeah, that was fun. But a young girl was even more fun. Pretty little runaway had no idea what she had gotten into when she climbed into his car. As he took his time tying her up, he smiled and ran his hand through her platinum blonde hair from time to time. He had her restrained at the wrists, the elbows, the ankle and knee, legs spread wide, straining the crotch of her cotton jersey pants.

The hair was silky, soft, straight as could be. She wasn't a real blonde—he'd already checked. The wispy little curls between her legs were a dark brown. But the blonde locks did look good on her.

As her eyes finally started to flutter open, he rested a hand on her belly and crouched down by her side. He propped his chin on the bed so that his face was next to hers. He wanted to be the first thing she saw when she came to.

Appropriate, since he planned on being the last thing she ever saw as well.

First there was confusion. The nerves and anxiety. As she started trying to move her arms and legs, she realized she was tied down, and that was when the fun began. As the terror entered her eyes, a pleased smile spread across his face. "Morning, sweetheart. Didn't anybody ever tell you not to go hitchhiking?"

She opened her mouth to scream and he just laughed.

"Nobody close enough to hear you, sweetie. They never heard the others. They won't hear you," he told her, leaning close so that his nose brushed against hers.

She recoiled into the mattress and screamed, the sound high and terrified. Pleased, he sat back on his heels to listen and watch.

଼

Mike felt the cool brush of the woman's body against his own as he hugged her. He never knew what to say to them, never understood if what he did was the right thing. But so far, this time, it seemed to be the right thing.

"I'll try to help her," he said.

She smiled up at him.

"Who is he?" he asked quietly. "Can you tell me?"

That was when she retreated. The minute he mentioned the man who had killed her, the ghost faded away. Fear crowded her mind and she fled.

Shoving a hand through his hair, he spun away, kicking a rock. Lucas was watching him from a distance. *"She's young."* Anger colored his voice, turned it into a thunderous crash that boomed through his mind as he spoke to Michael.

Sourly, Mike muttered, "Too many of them are."

*"You can't keep doing this, Mikey. Looking for killers, talking to ghosts."* Lucas looked at Mike, his eyes concerned, his mouth turned down in a familiar scowl. Mike had heard this song and dance before and it would end the same way it always did. Stopping wasn't an option.

Just like leaving wasn't an option for Lucas.

"Then why don't you give me a break—you talk to me nonstop."

Lucas grinned. *"I'm an exception. We're family."*

Slanting him an evil look, Mike started to prowl the grounds. He'd seen the yellow police tape but he'd also seen too many cases where small things had been missed. He needed something small—

something the killer had brushed up against could lead him right to the bastard.

It wouldn't take much. Hell, a rock that the killer had kicked as he dumped the body. Mike could lift a psychic impression as easily as a crime scene unit lifted fingerprints. But nearly an hour later—he had to admit, the whole place was virtually null. The killer had been very, very careful.

There wasn't a single thing that Mike could see to trace him.

At least not here. There would be something, though. There always was. All Mike had to do was wait. He just hoped it happened before another woman was killed.

ଔ

Daisy had to stifle the urge to snarl in pure frustration as the last possible lead she had on the killer who had killed four women in her town came up empty. Nothing. Yes, Kelsey Morrow told her, she *had* seen a car that night before she called him. But it was so dark…and she couldn't tell a Trans Am from a Camry, Kelsey relayed mournfully. She thought it was a four door—maybe. And the color was dark. But dark blue, dark green, gray…black…

*Damn* it. Daisy suspected it could have been a Pinto painted with black and white pinstripes, and Kelsey wouldn't have remembered. It could have been a vintage Mustang convertible in pristine condition, and Kelsey wouldn't have noticed.

Why, on earth, did the one woman who had seen the probable killer have to be Kelsey?

She was a sweet enough girl, and Daisy loved her dearly—after all, they were stepsisters.

But Kelsey was an airhead. Talking to her made Daisy as dizzy as a whirlwind. Daisy tugged on her braid in a gesture born of nervous habit as she muttered to herself, lowering her gaze back to the papers, reports and pictures spread out in front of her.

An hour later, she had poured through the scant file on Tanya Dourant and she came back to the conclusion that she had already reached.

Taken from her home, late at night, no signs of struggle in the house—and on the one night that her husband had been out bowling like he did every Wednesday.

She had known her killer.

Of course, they lived in Mitchell, for crying out loud. The small town in Indiana had less than a thousand who lived inside the city limits. Several hundred more in the county, outside the city limits. Almost everybody knew the other, at least at a glance. And Tanya was a nurse for the town's sole pediatrician. So she knew almost everybody. Damn it all.

Thirty-three, sweet, funny, good with kids…and dead.

Some son of a bitch had bled her like a damned pig.

Rubbing her thumb along one of the pictures, she studied it. That bright, happy grin made her heart hurt. Thinking about those little kids, asking for Mama day after day, and Daddy having to explain she wasn't ever coming home again.

Fury pulsed through her and she shoved back from the chair, pacing the small office and turning it over in her mind.

"Something. Has to be something," she muttered. Gritting her teeth, she lowered herself back into the chair and grabbed the first thing that came to hand. It was a crime scene photo of the empty field where Tanya's body had been dumped.

"Waste of time, going out there again." Then she shrugged and stood, grabbing her jacket on her way out the door.

Not that staying in the office was terribly productive right now.

The road was paved up until about a mile from the field. Tanya had been found by some hunters, a week after being reported missing. The hunters had known who it was. Daisy had seen the knowledge, the fury, the shock, in their eyes as they led her back out there.

As Daisy had expected, the official cause of death was hypovolemic shock, caused by massive blood loss. There had been thirty-six cuts, all inflicted by the same blade. Most likely the same knife that had been used on the other victims. They had all been cut thirty-six times as well. There was nothing careless or uncontrolled. The victims hadn't been stabbed violently, but cut with a careful precision.

Also like the others, Tanya had been raped. He had also spent some time strangling her. He'd squeezed her throat until she blacked out from the lack of oxygen and then he'd let her go. Let her wake up. And then he'd start all over again.

All of that, and he hadn't left a single sign of himself. Not a hair follicle, not a bit of skin under the fingernails, not a drop of semen or blood. He left nothing and Daisy had come up with nothing.

The instincts that had helped her nab some of the biggest drug runners in Louisville had deserted her. Not even a quiver as she walked the trail back to the field. Her gut had been playing tricks on her for a while, but now it was like she was working blind. No gut urges, no hunches to follow.

Just four dead bodies…and a stranger standing in the meadow where the last body was found.

It was the guy from the diner. He stood there, facing away from her, staring down at the ground. There was a knapsack slung over one big shoulder. It had a worn look to it, like it had been used a lot. Other than the bag, his hands were empty. But his clothes were dusty, like he had been kicking around the field for quite a while.

Twilight was starting to gleam gold on the horizon as Daisy calmly shifted the gun she wore inside her jacket. Hadn't ever gotten used to wearing a holster at her waist the way her predecessor had. Too many years working in narcotics, she supposed.

"You're on private property, pal," she said levelly.

The blue eyes that cut her way were the color of the sky just before sunrise. Deep, dark blue. And cool. Very cool. She hadn't noticed the color of his eyes back at the diner. Neither had she realized just how very…*large* he was.

Six feet four, easy. Shoulders that would have done a linebacker proud. High cheekbones and a chiseled chin. The only things that saved him from being too pretty were his hard, unsmiling mouth and his eyes. He had the saddest eyes that Daisy had ever seen.

"I'm sorry," he said, his voice a low, easy drawl that spoke of the South. "Just out seeing the sights. Saw the road. I wanted to take a look around."

"Look for…what, exactly?" she asked, suspicion in her gut. Sad eyes or not, there was no way he had just happened upon this place. The field was too damn far out for somebody to stumble on to it. The path to it was overgrown and unless somebody knew it was there, it wasn't going to be easy to find.

He lifted the bag at his side and smiled, but it wasn't a real smile. It wasn't reflected in his eyes, or on his face. Just a polite little smile to set people at ease, she suspected. But she wasn't put at ease. Not at all.

"Scenery. I'm an amateur photographer. On vacation, wanted

to find someplace quiet." His voice was soothing, the kind of voice that tended to reassure people.

Daisy wasn't looking for reassurance. She was looking for answers and she wanted to know what in the hell he was doing standing in the middle of her crime scene.

For a brief second, she entertained the possibility that this was her guy. It wasn't unusual for killers to revisit crime scenes—could explain why he was at the site where they'd found Tanya. He definitely had the weird, mysterious vibe to him. But it wasn't him. She didn't know why he was here, but it wasn't because he wanted to see if his victim had been found yet.

So instead of calling for back up, she just said, "Mitchell has plenty of nice places. And a lot of them aren't on private property. Maybe you should find of one of them."

That same polite little smile, and he nodded. "Of course. Hope I didn't cause trouble, Sheriff," he said. And then he was gone, moving past her on incredibly silent feet.

Daisy fought not to scowl as he headed for the trees, that black bag slung over his shoulders, his hands tucked into his pockets, broad shoulders straining at the seams of his worn denim shirt.

*Nice ass.*

Then she mentally slapped herself across the head, turning back to study the field with narrowed eyes.

She slid her gaze back in the direction where that sexy stranger had disappeared. Blowing a breath out, she started to jog across the field, catching sight of that faded blue denim. "Hey…hold up a minute."

Michael stopped in his tracks and raised his eyes heavenward as the woman's voice drifted to him.

*"Should have split when ya had the chance,"* Lucas said, a grin curving up his mouth. He was standing in the middle of the path. The lower half of his body was lost to sight. A big oak had fallen down some time ago and was blocking a lot of the path. Lucas looked like he was standing inside the oak. His upper body was transparent but it took on a more solid look every time he spoke. As he winked at Michael, he could have almost passed for something other than a ghost. *"I will tell ya, she is a looker."*

"Hmmm," Michael murmured. He turned around and watched the pretty sheriff approach. Nope, he couldn't disagree. She had a head full of riotous golden brown curls and a direct hazel stare that was kind of uncommon in a woman. Of course, since she was a cop, that direct stare shouldn't be a surprise. She had a small, straight nose, high cheekbones and her eyebrows were so dark a brown they appeared black.

Her body was a compact, deadly package of curves and muscles. She looked incredibly soft and incredibly strong. Definitely a lethal package. As she moved, he caught a quick glimpse of the shoulder holster under her jacket and he imagined she was every bit as competent with that gun as she looked.

Michael had always had a weakness for women like her—confident, composed, strong and sexy as all get out. She wouldn't mind if a man opened the door for her but at the same time, she probably handled a weapon better than most men did.

He heard Lucas snickering and he gave his brother a silent warning. The last thing he needed was to make the pretty sheriff think he was just a little too strange. That sort of thing could land him in jail, considering the shit they had going on here.

He met her eyes, arching a brow, keeping his expression blank, forcing his mouth into a curious smile. "Ma'am?"

"Just occurred to me. I haven't seen you around before," she said. "Well, at the diner. But eh…other than that, well, you know, Mitchell doesn't see too much in the way of tourists or travelers. Been in town long?"

He shrugged, keeping his gaze from cutting to his brother as Lucas murmured, *"She's onto us, pal."*

Michael said, "I drove in yesterday. Slept at the Spring's Inn. Was planning on heading out today, but then I decided to wait a few days. It's quiet here. I like the quiet."

"Yes. I do, too. I work real hard to keep it quiet. I'm Daisy Crandall. The sheriff here. We've been having some trouble lately. Strangers in town probably aren't going to help people rest easier. Care to give me your name? What you've been doing the past few days?"

"Michael," he sighed out, rubbing his hand across his eyes. "Michael O'Rourke. And until four days ago, I was in Philadelphia. I'm on vacation for the next few weeks."

"Taking…pictures?" she supplied, arching a skeptical brow.

"If I feel the need," he said shortly.

"And what is it you do in Philadelphia? You don't exactly sound like a Yankee to me. Lived there long?"

Damn. Cops. He wasn't in the mood to lie to her, although he could fabricate a very believable, very plausible story. Still, if he thought she'd believe him, he would have done it. But she wouldn't believe him.

She'd know he was lying and that would just make more trouble. So instead, he hedged a little, telling her the truth without really telling her anything. "I don't live there. I was there for a job," he said, clenching his jaw.

"A job, huh?" She propped her hands on her waist—a move that was intended to let him see the gun tucked into its holster, and the shiny badge on her belt. She had her intimidation tactics down pretty well. "What kind of job?"

Michael debated on what to tell her. Finally, he blew out a sigh and shook his head. Oz was going to shoot him. His boss wasn't very fond of having people outside the unit know about any of the agents. Of course, if this cop started running his name, she was going to find him in areas where all sorts of bad things happened.

When he stayed silent, she glanced at the black strap hanging from his shoulder. "Let me guess…photography?"

That little smirk of a smile on her lips probably did all sorts of things to piss people off. And he was sure that was exactly the point. "No." He tapped his fingers against the wallet he kept in his front pocket. "Mind?"

"That depends on what you have in your pocket," she replied drolly.

"ID."

Her eyes narrowed and she said, "Why do I have the feeling you already know the drill? One hand only…use two fingers."

"Well, you are quick," he drawled, drawing the wallet from his pocket and handing it over before letting his hand fall back to his side.

"FBI?" she said, that brow inching up higher, her voice thick with doubt.

"Sort of. A division. I was there on assignment, finished it. Now I'm on vacation," he said.

"Says you're from Tennessee. It's been my experience that most Southerners are a little more talkative than you," the sheriff said, still holding his ID in her hand as she studied him with very cynical eyes. "Don't suppose there is somebody I can call to verify this information?"

Behind him, he heard Lucas snickering. *"I can verify,"* his brother said. *"Lot of help that will be though."*

*"Will you just shut up?"* Michael thought sourly. Lucas just continued to grin at him. His brother had always had a weird sense of humor. Being dead twenty years had only made it more so.

Michael ran a hand through his hair and muttered, "Oz is going to kill me."

"Oz?"

Okay, so she was expecting either a drugged out rock and roll singer, or an actor with a quirky smile that just liked to shape shift into a werewolf. *I watch too much TV*. The low, smooth contralto on the other end of the line was definitely not what Daisy had expected when Michael scrawled out the number and agreed to ride with her into town.

"Yes," Elise Oswald said levelly. "O'Rourke is one of my men. I'm kind of curious as why you are calling me. My people generally are rather closed mouthed."

"Oh, he's closed mouthed, all right. But he happened into a town in Indiana where we've been having some kind of serious problems," Daisy said. As she spoke, she tapped her pen on a pad of paper, then circled the woman's name, the phone number, drawing a line under it. She doodled a little more, adding a triangle under the name, then jotting the sexy agent's name down as well.

"Indiana." Oswald repeated it slowly, like she was speaking a foreign language. Then she made a little humming noise and murmured, "So that's where he disappeared to."

"You been looking for him?" Daisy asked, giving him a wary glance. She shifted in her seat a little, making sure she could grab her weapon if she needed it. He watched her the entire time, with that little half smile on his mouth.

"Not exactly. O'Rourke made it clear he wasn't interested in being found any time soon. Please let him know that he is officially on a leave of absence for the next month, so if he would turn his pager back on, I'd be most appreciative."

"Riiigggghhhttt…" Daisy drawled. "Why don't you tell me a little more about him, Ms. Oswald."

On the other end of the phone, Elise laughed. "Call me Elise or Oz. I rarely respond to Ms." She made that little humming sound again and murmured, "Now let me see. About O'Rourke. There's not too much that I can share, but O'Rourke has a habit of happening into places where all sorts of trouble is going on. That's one of the reasons he's with me." She sounded just a little amused as she said it.

"You like troublemakers?" Daisy asked curiously.

With a laugh, Oswald said, "Hardly. What I like is the fact that he always ends up where he is needed. There's a problem, he finds it, solves it, moves on to another."

Dryly, Daisy said, "How nice for you. But I don't need a problem solver. I just need you to verify he was in Philadelphia…like for last week?"

"I can verify that."

Eyeing the silent stranger in front of her, Daisy scowled. "Can you expand on that a little? Some more detail?"

"No, Sheriff. I can't. You asked for verification, not detail."

Elise Oswald spoke with a cool amusement that only added to Daisy's irritation. Patience and professionalism took a quick leap out the window. "Look, lady," she snapped. "I've got four dead bodies and I just found your boy standing in a very remote area where the latest one was found. That's a little strange, don't you think?"

Elise Oswald's evasiveness sure as hell wasn't helping Daisy's mindset either. Oddly, though, the lack of answers didn't matter. Michael O'Rourke wasn't a killer. She knew it with a certainty that went clear down to her bones.

Oswald started to laugh. "Not if you know O'Rourke. You have absolutely no idea how many strange places with all sorts of bad things that he just happens to walk into. And if you have O'Rourke there, you should know, he's not a boy, mine or otherwise."

Daisy fell silent, staring at the ID in front of her. Instincts, long since fallen silent, started to scream at her and the hair on the back of her neck stood on end. "Exactly what does that mean?"

On the other end of the line, Oswald simply said, "Could mean a lot of things—could mean he just has a habit of ending up in weird places. Could be something else. But like I said, he was here, on assignment, last week. And every week before for the past several months."

"Doing what?"

"Now that…I can't answer." And the line went dead.

Slowly, Daisy hung up the phone and sat back in the chair. Looking up, she stared at Michael O'Rourke. She did have to agree with Oswald on one thing—Michael O'Rourke was no boy.

Dark, broody looks, lean powerful body and a mouth that looked like it had been made for kissing. Sleepy looking blue eyes, that deep slow voice with its faint Southern accent—the man was a walking, talking dream. Sure as hell nothing boy-like about him.

He sat in the chair across from her desk, his hands resting on his thighs. His bag was sitting at the desk out front where he'd surrendered it without protest. He didn't fidget, didn't do anything that portrayed any kind of nerves, guilt or a need to intimidate.

There was nothing he had done that shouted *threat.*

Yet, everything about him made Daisy aware of just that. He wasn't a man to be tangled with.

Meeting those dark blue eyes, she pushed his wallet back across the desk. With a polite, professional smile, Daisy said, "You're clear. But you might not want to hang around town, Agent O'Rourke. People are getting antsy. Having a stranger around isn't going to help any."

She arched a brow at him, angled her head to door. "You can go."

Without comment, he stood and tucked away his wallet. He turned to the door but instead of leaving, he just stood there. When he turned back around to look at her, his eyes were hooded. "Curious. What's going on around here? People are edgy. Even for uptight Yankees," he said with a twist of his lips.

"None of your concern, Agent O'Rourke. Especially if you were just in the field for the scenery," she said, tongue in cheek.

*"Don't,* man."

Michael ignored Lucas' intense voice as he picked up the heavy rock that sat on Sheriff Dasynda Crandall's desk. It was an amethyst. The purple spikes that stood out from the inside caught the light as he shifted it back and forth.

*"Don't do this, Mike. If she doesn't believe you, you're going to find your ass thrown in jail."*

Focusing his mind toward Lucas, he replied, *"And if I don't, somebody else dies. I can't let that happen. That woman in the field asked for help—I can't walk away."*

Mike blocked his brother from his thoughts and concentrated

on the crystal in his hands as he started to speak. "A woman was found in that field," he said softly. The images rolled in his mind like a silent movie, her body being dragged out of the trunk, thrown on the ground…a wood cabin, a hand closing around her throat, the silver flash as a knife lifted and descended, over and over. The slow trickle of blood. The eventual weakness.

"But she wasn't killed there."

Daisy sat up and he watched as the flat, blank look entered her eyes. Cop look. He knew one, had practiced and perfected his own, even though he wasn't exactly a cop. At least, Mike didn't think of himself as one.

"Okay. Care to tell me how you know any of that?" she asked tightly.

"There was a cabin," he said distantly, hardly even aware of her question. He continued to stare down at the amethyst but instead of the pretty purple spikes, he saw wooden plank floors and wooden walls, a narrow bed, rusty bloodstains on the floor. "He killed her there. She knew him."

Daisy stood up so quick her chair toppled over. Her eyes flashed with fury, the professional cop gone in the heat of anger. "All right, slick, I don't give a damn if you do have an alibi, if you don't tell me how you know that, you can look forward to spending some time behind bars," she snapped.

The jagged points of the amethyst pressed into his palm as he murmured, "Your dad gave you this. He was a cop, too, wasn't he? Died in the line of duty—drug deal. You almost left your badge behind when that happened."

Blood roared in his ears as he felt the surge of emotions rolling from her. Confusion, the first wink of understanding, smashed out by her disbelief. They never wanted to believe. Lifting his head, he stared into her wide, angry eyes.

"How in the hell do you know that?" she demanded.

The smile that curved his lips now was a real one, cynical, just a slight twist of his lips, as he shrugged. "I think you already know."

Daisy felt the knowledge slam into her like an uppercut, shock and disbelief warring in her mind for supremacy. This wasn't possible. Not possible.

"He has another."

Slowly, she leaned forward and planted her hands on the table.

"What?"

"A girl."

"Not possible. If a girl was missing in Mitchell, especially with this going on, her family would have already called," Daisy said flatly. One of the nice things about small towns.

"She isn't from here. A girl. Walking down the highway," Michael O'Rourke said, staring into her eyes. "Long blonde hair—not her real color. She's…she's not well. Bad heart."

She watched him with disbelief as his lashes lowered, hiding his eyes for a minute. When he looked back at her, she felt the power of that gaze like a punch in the solar plexus. That mild blue gaze was no longer quite so mild.

His eyes seemed to glow.

Daisy blew out a shaky breath and turned away from him for a minute while she tried to calm her rattled emotions. The deep breath didn't help and neither did staring out the plate glass window that took up most of the back wall of her little office. She was too aware of him. She could feel his eyes boring into her back, waiting to see what she did. How she reacted.

But Daisy wasn't sure how to react to this. Suddenly, this case had become a whole different ball game.

଼

Whoever the killer was knew small town life, knew when to play his cards and when to hold his hand. He also knew how to hide his tracks. How to blend in. He lived here. She knew it in her gut.

It was somebody that she knew, probably somebody she'd grown up with. Most serial killers were men, usually under the age of forty, which put him right in her age bracket.

Son of a bitch.

Lowering her eyes, she looked at the gruesome pictures one last time and silently promised yet again, *I will find you.*

"How many?" Michael asked quietly.

Cutting the man at her side a narrow look, she said sarcastically, "Don't you know?"

"Doesn't work that way," he said, lifting one shoulder.

"How does it work?" she asked, crossing her arms over her

stomach.

"Ever seen *The Sixth Sense*?"

Her nose wrinkled. Images of animated corpses walking around filled her head. "Ewww…" Then she looked back at the pictures of the dead victims. "Dead people?"

"My gift. They don't look like that—they look however they last see themselves. They usually know they are dead and if they don't, they figure it out pretty quick. That doesn't always help though," Michael said. His voice was expressionless, his blue eyes blank, and just blue now, no longer glowing. "They talk to me. The woman who was in the field…" His gaze drifted over her shoulder and she shivered. He was looking at somebody. "She sees the girl. But she's confused. Still doesn't understand what happened. She knows somebody killed her, and she's scared. Hurt."

"Sees what girl?" Daisy asked warily. This all felt surreal. But not for a moment did she think he was lying. She hadn't ever met a person she believed more.

"The one he has now. She's blonde, young…pale," Michael murmured. "I can see her through your friend's eyes…Tanya…yes, Tanya. I can see her through Tanya's eyes."

A shiver raced down Daisy's back as he lifted his head, turning it to stare to Daisy's right, at a point by the window. His eyes seemed to lock with something, but the room was empty, save for them.

"Are you…talking to Tanya now?"

A smile edged up the corners of his mouth and he shook his head. "No. She can't come here. She's trapped there, in the field. And in the cabin where he killed her."

"I need to know more about this cabin."

Michael's eyes closed and she watched as he sighed, his shoulders slumping just a little. "I can't tell you more…she only saw the inside of it. She never saw a clock, never saw the sun shining through the window. Pine…she could smell pine trees. She's blocked out his face."

"What do you mean blocked it out?" Daisy asked, scowling.

"Blocked it. She's too afraid of him, what he did—she won't think about it. And I can't make her do it until she's ready." His voice trailed off. Then he shook his head and looked at her, his eyes blank and empty. "I can't tell you anything that could help. Not right now, not yet. When she's ready, she'll help us. But right now's too afraid."

Tears burned her eyes. *God... Tanya...*

A hand came up, squeezing her shoulder. "I'm sorry."

Shrugging away from him, she closed her eyes. "I thought once a person died, they were beyond that," she said, forcing the words past the knot in her throat. God, she prayed, she hoped.

God, how she could face any of these families knowing that the poor victims might be stuck here...

"A lot of the time, they can move on. Sometimes they can't." Michael's gaze flickered back to the window and she frowned, looking at the window then at him.

"What stops them?"

"Life. Sometimes they see or feel right before they die—" his voice broke off.

"And what's keeping Tanya here?" she demanded. "Damn it, you don't have any idea what he did to her!"

He lifted haunted eyes to her face. "Yes, I do. You don't. You saw her body. You didn't feel it. She can't talk to you. You can't feel her fear. You aren't trapped inside that cabin. She is. And she's terrified she won't be able to keep him from hurting the girl that's there now."

# CHAPTER THREE

Daisy tried to dismiss it.

Tried very hard.

But she couldn't even find it in her to *doubt* him, much less totally dismiss him. Over the next hour, she flipped through the flyers, studying them, looking for a young, pale blonde.

There were a number of them. Had he taken one of them?

She sifted out the five blondes who had disappeared recently, tossing the rest into a basket on her desk, rubbing her temple as she read the names. Should be easy. Bad heart. Hair wasn't the natural color.

A breeze blew through the room and she absently rubbed her arms, not noticing as one of the flyers in the basket drifted to the floor.

A young girl, teenaged, pale skinned, her brunette hair waving around her narrow face, stared up from the grainy photo. The words *urgent* right below her picture would have caught Daisy's eye if she had seen it.

When somebody called into her office fifteen minutes later, she pushed the flyers aside, scowling as Deputy Jake Morris grinned at her from the doorway. "This is the third time Myrtle has called the office. She'll only talk to you, Daisy," he said, laughter dancing in his eyes.

"I can't help that some stray dogs are shitting in her petunias," Daisy muttered, smoothing a hand across her hair, tucking a stray lock behind her ear.

"Roses. It's her rose bushes this time," he said helpfully. "You going to talk to her?"

Sourly, Daisy muttered, "Why in the hell should I? She'll just keep calling until I go out there."

"Should I tell her that you're on your way?"

"Yes." Lifting her eyes skyward, she murmured, "Give me patience."

ଓଃ

Twenty minutes later, Daisy repeated, for the fifth time, "Mrs. Morrow, please, if you will tell me what the dog looked like, maybe we can figure out if it has an owner. But unless you *see* the dog, there's not much I can do."

Daisy covered her nose as Myrtle Morrow waved a blue plastic grocery bag in front of her, the stench of the dog poop inside the bag drifting out to flood her nose. "You're telling me you won't help me?" Mrs. Morrow demanded in strident tones.

"I'm saying I can't—not unless you can at least tell me what the dog looks like," Daisy said, trying not to grit her teeth. She didn't know if she had succeeded though.

"It's a *dog*!"

Daisy rubbed her temple and said, "Listen. We have more than three hundred and thirty three dogs in the town limits. I checked. And more strays than I care to think about. So unless you have an idea to figure out which of those three hundred plus pooches crapped in the rose bushes, I don't know what I can do."

A chill ran down her spine, making her shiver. The skin on the back of her neck prickled, and the feeling of being watched settled within her. Blinking, she forced herself to focus on Myrtle, taking her arm and guiding her back to her porch. She made the appropriate sympathetic noises as the old woman brandished the poop bag and gestured wildly toward her roses.

"I'll find the dog. I'll stay up night and day if I have to," Myrtle muttered, staring at the bag and sulking.

"And as soon as you can tell me what it looks like, I'll do what I can," Daisy promised.

Which wouldn't be much, because Myrtle would most likely

describe a dog that matched the description of half the strays and registered pets in town. But at least Daisy was able to walk away from her house. Sliding into her car, she checked the rearview mirror. Nobody around that she could see. But somebody was watching her. She could feel it.

It felt like somebody was trying to puzzle her out.

But there was nobody even around, that she could see. Myrtle lived at the end of a cul-de-sac and there was only one other house on her street. The Busseys were out of town on vacation and Myrtle had most likely gone inside to sulk some more over her roses.

With a sigh, she started the car and headed back to town. "I'm losing my mind."

ઙ૪

*"She's a good cop."*

Michael closed his eyes as Lucas wavered into view.

"Leave her alone, Lucas," he said tiredly. It was a waste of time. Lucas was feeling the need to investigate, which meant he was going to do everything *but* leave her alone.

Not good.

He sensed something about Daisy Crandall that made his skin itch. She had believed him all too easily. Cops didn't do that. And it didn't matter that her badge said *County Sheriff*. Still a cop.

She should have been a lot more skeptical.

The only reason that made sence as to why she didn't scoff at him…she knew he wasn't lying.

Some people had that knowledge, the ability to look at somebody and know whether that person was telling them lies—or truth. She had known. Plain and simple. And if she could sense truth, she could possibly sense other things. He'd rather she not know about the ghost that followed him.

*"I like her."*

Now Michael frowned. Staring at Lucas, he cocked a brow, waiting. Lucas hadn't ever said that about anybody before. He wouldn't like somebody he couldn't trust. He'd been very cautious in life about who he cared for—death had only enhanced that.

Lucas shrugged as he met his brother's stare. It was an odd gesture, one that made his mostly solid image ripple for a moment and Michael saw the outline of the dresser behind Lucas for the briefest second. *"She's…solid,"* Lucas finally said. *"And sad. There's something broken inside her."*

Michael felt his heart clench at Lucas' words. Yes, he had sensed the grief inside the pretty, sloe-eyed woman. It had left an urge inside him, to go to her and cuddle her against him, stroke away the bleak look in her pretty brown eyes. "Nothing I can do about that," he murmured. He wished he had just moved on. There were complications here that he didn't need—complications that went beyond the ghost of a murdered woman and a missing runaway.

But she pulled at him…not just the ghost.

The sheriff.

Too often, the only people that could hold his interest were the dead. They whispered to him at night, surrounded him during the day. But the living, they rarely held any interest for him.

He felt her determination to find the murderer, a deep, steady intent that all but colored the air around her. Solid. Yes…true blue. Loyal, determined, steady, through and through.

Michael couldn't walk away until he knew there would be no more ghosts behind him when he left. Which meant stopping the killer.

Running his tongue along his teeth, he studied the articles in front of him, sifting through to find the earliest one. Six dead women. Going back a year and half. The last two had both been killed within the past four months. The killer was escalating. They developed a taste for it, a need. Time passed and they had to kill more often, more frequently.

More violently.

Were there only the four? Or had he hidden some of the victims?

Areas like this were thick with woods and valleys, easy places to hide bodies. These four had been local. But Michael knew there was one out there that wasn't from around here. A runaway…somebody barely more than a child. If he had taken one runaway, he'd likely taken others.

So possibly more murders than they knew about.

Rubbing his thumb across his chin, he contemplated the grainy picture in the paper. Pretty. Young…in her twenties. But the second one was in her early forties. And then a college coed who'd been home on summer break. The fourth one, the nurse, the ghost he had met earlier—28, married, mom with kids. Only thing they really had in common…they were female and white.

No pattern. That made it harder to pin things down.

There was something else that had to link them.

"What's the damned link?" he muttered, shoving a hand through his hair.

*"You know, some people just like to kill."*

"Yeah, but they usually have a preferred sort of victim," Mike said absently.

*"You've become too much like a cop."*

Mike smiled. "I don't know what else there is left for me to be, Lucas."

A cool breeze drifted through the room.

Feeling the heavy weight of emotion that seemed to roll from Lucas, he looked up. "It's not your fault," he said quietly. "And this isn't a bad rap, you know."

*"You wade through the shittiest type of scum known to man, Mikey. You've put yourself inside the heads of monsters—I see how sick it makes you. I know how angry it makes you. I know it hurts. And you want me to buy that it's not a bad rap."* Lucas shook his head. His eyes were so full of grief, it hurt to even look at his brother, but Mike wouldn't look away.

"Yeah. I want you to believe it." Scrubbing his hands over his face, he sighed. Pushing back from the small desk, Mike started to pace the tight confines of the hotel room. "Yeah. I've had to deal with shit. But you and me…we've been doing that all our lives. It's not like I don't know how to handle it."

*"I should have tried harder. We should have left sooner."*

"Neither of us could have known how low she would have stooped. Or what kind of messes she had gotten involved in," Mike said quietly.

Lucas spun away. The force of rage flooding him had made his image wavery and Mike could barely see him. *"I should have. I knew her—I knew what kind of scum she was involved in, knew better than you what she was capable of. I was supposed to protect you, Mikey. I failed. I shouldn't have let this happen to you."*

"It happened to *you*," Mike said.

*"It happened to us both."*

That stopped him in mid-stride. He turned around, looking

across the room at his brother. "Guess it did. And it happened for a reason. If it hadn't..." Grisly images, things he'd rather forget, rolled through his mind. No, he didn't want to remember many things that he'd seen in the past ten or fifteen years of his life. But lives had been saved because of it, killers had been stopped. "There's a man sitting in jail right now because of what happened to me. His last victim didn't die. We got to him before he could hurt her. You know what? I couldn't have stopped him if I was your everyday average Jones, Lucas. It may not be the easiest thing to live with, but I'd rather have some bad nights and know that bastard will never kill anybody again, then to change it."

*"Don't you think you've done enough, Mike?"*

Focusing on the papers in front of him, he blew out a breath. "No. There's a girl out there, Lucas. A kid. He has a kid. And I'm not going to stop until I've stopped him."

*"And then there will be another. And another...and another. When will it ever be enough?"*

"That's the way it works."

As Lucas' presence faded away, Mike focused again on the information in front of him.

*You hurt that girl, you son of a bitch, and you're going to die.*

ꙮ

Tanya felt it in her heart when the girl died.

The blackness that surrounded the cabin expanded and she wanted to flee, but at the same time, her own anger kept her chained. She had hoped...had prayed...the man, she'd thought he would help. He hadn't, though.

Tanya waited and waited but he never came and now it was too late.

Terror welled inside. Only one thing caused that. *Him*—the killer. The killer was coming. *Her* killer. *"My killer,"* she whispered.

Her throat felt tight. It was weird. She could still feel things. When Michael had touched her earlier, she had felt it. His arms had felt bizarrely hot, like he'd had a fever. It had been get a shock, all over her body and it left her skin buzzing and burning, in a very, very painful way.

Did she feel cold to him?

She wanted to run. But the only place she could go was the field. She already knew that. And that was just as bad as here. Every time she ended up there, she kept remembering what she had seen. She'd run there the first time. Because *he* had come here. To clean up after he had killed her. She ran, and she found herself. She saw what he did to her. Seeing it was just as bad as feeling it, in a different way.

Tanya had watched as two childhood friends led the police to her body. She was stuck there, watching as Daisy and her deputies searched for clues that would lead to him. Deep inside, Tanya knew that she knew who he was. But it was like she'd closed the door on his memory, on his face. She couldn't look at him. Wouldn't.

The terror inside grew so thick it was choking her, flooding her. She couldn't keep doing that. Needed to see him. Had to. So she could tell Michael. Michael was there to help. He could tell Daisy. God…Daisy. Tears squeezed out of her eyes and Tanya had to bite back the scream that was building in her throat. They had been planning to go into town and watch a movie. Get a few drinks…just have a girl day.

They wouldn't do that now. There would never be another girl day. She'd never take her daughter shopping for that dress. Amy's first big dance was next month and Tanya wasn't ever going to see her, wouldn't be able to take pictures… She'd lost out on all of it.

Rage started to edge back the terror even though the blackness moved closer. *He* was moving closer. Turning, Tanya stared at the still body of the girl lying tied to the cot. *"I'm so sorry, sweetie,"* she whispered.

The girl just lay there.

Her body was still covered. She hadn't been battered…beaten…cut, or raped. Not yet. Tanya couldn't help but feel a little jealous. "You got off easy, baby. I wish I'd died before he touched me."

☙❧

He felt the voice. At first, he was convinced it was his own imagination, but then, as it continued to echo inside his mind, he had to wonder.

And there was a stranger in town—one who had been seen talking to the sheriff. One who had been seen out where Tanya's body had been found. He was a big, mean looking bastard with sharp eyes.

He hadn't heard that voice, either, not until that man had shown up. Now it was like he wouldn't shut up. This was not good. Not at all. As the echo of the words ran through the man's mind, repeating themselves over and over, he started to worry.

*Let her go… Let her go now, and maybe I won't kill you when I find you.*

Shaken, he jogged out of the house and leaped into his truck, whipping it around and speeding for the cabin where the girl was kept. She lay there, sweet, innocuous…and dead.

He bellowed with rage, launching himself to the cot and grabbing one wrist. A pulse…there would be a pulse. She wasn't dead, she was playacting to try and get free. Stupid little bitch. She was going to pay for this. Damn it, nobody cheated him. Nobody.

But the skin was cool—she had a pasty, grayish blue cast to her skin and her eyes stared sightlessly up at the ceiling. There was a weird little curl to her lips, almost a smile. Mocking him.

She'd been dead a while.

He shot to his feet, pacing back and forth, dragging his hands through his hair and gnawing worriedly at his lower lip. What in the hell had happened? The ethyl chloride he'd used on her was harmless. And she'd woken up since then. What in the hell…

Spying her purse, he grabbed it and dumped it out. Hairspray, a comb, a cell phone with a dead battery, loose coins, two prescription bottles and a thick wad of cash. Something hit the floor with a musical clink and he knelt, eyeing the stainless steel bracelet with dread. The red caduceus winked up at him mockingly as he lifted it.

The medical terms didn't make much sense to him, the *V2* and the medical jargon was all but foreign to him. Except the words *cardiac murmur*—those words, he understood all too well.

Turning, he studied her face with disbelieving eyes.

She'd gone and had a fucking heart attack on him.

"You little bitch!" he screamed. "Bitch. Fucking bitch!"

He stood up and lashed out with his boot, kicking the cot. In a fit of fury, he stormed across the cabin, cussing furiously, completely unaware that he was being watched.

Tanya hovered in the corner. Her own fear was slowly dissipating, washing away as the sense of irony settled in. She stared at the two bottles of pills and at the bracelet, moving closer. He cut her off and she shied away automatically, but he still came close. He stilled though and she watched as he shivered. Smiling, she moved over to the spilled pile of drugs by the girl's purse.

*"Poor thing,"* she whispered. Died of a heart attack.

He came to an abrupt halt, staring around with wild eyes. "Who's there? Who the hell is that?"

Looking up, Tanya studied him. It was the first time she had consciously looked at him. His features came into focus… Recoiling in horror, she shied away, letting her mind blur his features again. *No…not ready…*part of her whispered. She wasn't ready to look at him. Wasn't ready to remember what he had done. How he had laughed when she screamed and cried.

But the other part of her thought logically. Realistically.

He heard her.

*"You can hear me,"* she said flatly.

"Who in the fuck is here?" he demanded. His eyes kept wheeling around in his head as he searched the room for her.

Slowly, Tanya stood, a smile curving her lips as she moved closer. Reaching out, she touched his cheek. *"Take a guess."*

ଓଃ

A cold touch drifted down his spine, bringing Michael out of his restless sleep. It wasn't the first time he had been woken up like this and he knew it wouldn't be the last. A restless spirit hovered around him and he swallowed back the furious shout that threatened to escape him. *Too late.* Bitter knowledge burned inside him but he clamped a tight lid on it.

The poor girl didn't need his anger.

"Hi," he said quietly, wondering if she would be stuck here, or if she was just a little lost.

There weren't any words from her. Just a sense of confusion.

"It's okay—takes a little time to move on sometimes," he said softly.

She sighed. He felt it like a breeze moving through the air. She was afraid, worried. She knew what had happened—she was angry, and she wanted her mother. Finally, images of her mom made her hurt enough, made her angry enough that she was able to speak. *"Why did I leave…what's going to happen to my mom? She'll never know."*

"I'm sorry."

*"What do I do? Am I stuck here?"*

At least this much, he could help with. "No…no, you're not stuck. You can move on any time you're ready to let go."

*"I can't go until I know Mom will be okay."*

Michael promised, "I'll make sure your mom knows that you've moved on. That's what I do."

There was the beauty of youth, though. Sometimes, they did still accept what you told them. It took a while to coax her to move along, but eventually she did. She started to see the white light—one thing that the movies had gotten right. She moved toward it and there was one less ghost in his life.

But that meant somewhere out there, a young woman lay dead.

*"You couldn't have just left."*

"Neither could you."

Lucas stood by the window, materializing out of thin air, his form more ghostly than normal. *"You make me seem a lot more altruistic than I am. I cared about two things when I was alive, Mike. Me. You. That was it."*

Walking past the window, Michael didn't spare his brother a glance as he said, "Don't give me that line. If you knew innocent girls were being killed, would you just walk away? This last one was just a girl. Younger than you were." Mike was quiet for a minute and then he looked back at Lucas. "People knew what she was doing to us, man. They knew what she tried to do to me. How many times did you have to save me from it, Lucas? Were there times that I didn't even know about?"

Lucas' silence was answer enough. Mike had always suspected it but now he knew. His mother had been willing to sacrifice Mike for Lucas' sake, but now he knew the truth. She would have sacrificed him to score some coke. Mike wanted to be angry but he realized he just didn't care.

"People knew. They walked away. Time after time. If somebody had done something, we might have made it out of there."

*"You did make it out of there. Hell, so did I. Just not quite the way I planned."*

Nausea churned in Michael's gut. "That's not funny, Lucas."

Lucas laughed bitterly. *"I wasn't trying to be funny, pal. But I* did *get out. You think I wanted to hang around there waiting until it was the* right *time to get away from her? Every second we hung around, you were in danger. And that last night, I could have killed her. What if they'd found you? We did get out. I'm just sorry it was hell on you for as long as it was."*

Hell—Dear God, that didn't even cover it. How many nights had he lain awake wondering if dawn would ever come, and the monsters would fade with the light, if the voices that whispered to him were demonic dreams manifested by his own mind or if they were real?

It had taken him years to come to grips with the fact that they were real. Even longer to not wake up terrified when that ghostly touch came on him at night.

He saw ghosts. They touched him, spoke to him, whispered to him—and begged him for help in finding their killers. He never saw those who passed peacefully at the sunset of their lives. Only those whose lives were ended far too early.

With a weary sigh, he flicked on the switch in the bathroom, squinting at the overly bright light . Turning on the water, he bent over and splashed it on his face until the rest of the cobwebs faded. With his hands braced on the tiled edges of the sink, he stared at his reflection. He was starting to look old. It wasn't lines on his face, though, or gray in his hair. His hair was still a deep, dark brown and the only lines on his face were the little ones fanning out from his eyes.

It was the eyes that made him look old.

*"You going to look for the girl? You never have that much luck finding them once they've passed on."*

Drying his face on the towel, Michael said, "I'm going to find the sheriff. Then I'll go out to the field. The lady there will know the girl's passed. If she's not ready to help now, she will be soon."

ଓଃ

Sarah's bark woke her up. Sitting up, Daisy whistled and the retriever obediently left the window and came over to her, ears perked and waiting. "Who's out there, girl?" she asked softly, dragging a hand through her hair. Her curls tangled around her fingers and she sighed. She'd been so damned tired, she'd gone to bed before her hair had dried all the way.

Bad move for a woman whose hair curled the way hers did.

She stood up and moved over to the window, peering through the blinds. The sleek little convertible moving up the road wasn't one she recognized. The full moon shining down was bright enough for her to see pretty well—buffed to a high shine, late model, and the top was down. She didn't know a person in town that owned that kind of car.

And since she didn't recognize it, Daisy had a good idea who it was.

FBI Agent Michael O'Rourke.

It was the middle of the night. She didn't have to be a cop to know it was a bad sign, an agent showing up on her front door this late. Turning away from the window, she moved to her dresser and pulled out a pair of jeans. Drawing them up over her hips, she grabbed the bra she draped over the foot of the bed and put it on. Just as the truck pulled up in front of the house, she tugged a skinny strapped tank top on. Glancing in the mirror, she made a face at her reflection. Her hair was a mess.

Making a side trip to the bathroom, she splashed some cold water on her face and slicked her damp hands over her hair. The door bell rang. Turning away from the mirror, she padded away out of the bathroom and down the hall.

Sarah waited patiently at the door, her liquid eyes black in the darkness. Reaching out, Daisy turned on the light, giving her eyes a second to adjust before looking through the Judas hole. "Out kind of late, aren't you?" she asked as she unlocked the chain to let him in.

His eyes were grim. There was a chill to his features that made her gut go cold. And suddenly, Daisy wished she had stayed in bed. Wouldn't have mattered though. She felt cold all over. A cop knew what was wrong when a person was woken up in the middle of the night. It was because somebody had died.

"Why are you here?" she asked softly, backing away from him. She rested her hips against the hall table and folded her arms around her chest.

"She's gone."

"Tanya?" Daisy asked, clenching her jaw.

"No…Tanya hasn't passed on yet," he said quietly. He continued to watch her closely and she saw the answer in his eyes.

Daisy had never seen anybody who looked as haunted as he did. She prayed she'd never see it again. Swallowing the knot in throat, she said huskily, "Then you're going to have to explain who you are talking about. Tanya is the only one who has died recently."

"I told you that he had taken somebody else."

It seemed like the pit of her belly dropped out. Closing her eyes, she said, "No. You said he just took her." One hand closed into a tight fist and she fought against the useless burst of fury. *No.*

"He didn't kill her. She died."

Perplexed, Daisy opened her eyes and glared at him. She shoved off the table and planted her hands on her hips. "Damn it, O'Rourke, you're not making much sense. Now granted, it is the middle of the night and I'm in dire need of a caffeine rush. But if you're going to come here and tell me that a girl is dead—" She clamped her mouth shut and hissed out a breath. She took a deep breath. Tried to think, turned his words over in her head. Nope. Still didn't make sense. Looking back at him, she said in a tight voice, "You need to remember something. I'm a cop. I'm the town sheriff. I take a dead girl pretty damned seriously. Especially since we have a killer using my town as his hunting ground."

His lashes lowered, hiding the haunting blue of his eyes. "She was sick—bad heart. I told you that. I think her heart gave out."

With that, he turned on his heel and started for the door.

"Hey!"

He paused, looking over his shoulder.

"Where in the hell do you think you're going?"

"Out to the field. Tanya might be ready to talk to me."

Propping her hands on her hips, Daisy stared at him. "Why? What changes things from this morning?"

"Because a girl is dead," Michael said, his tone patient, as though he was talking to a small child.

"Yeah and this morning, talking might have *saved* her."

Michael's lips curled in a sad smile. "I don't think so—you don't understand, Sheriff. The deceased, they are like kids. Like a young one, scared, confused and alone in the dark. She couldn't this morning—it just wasn't time, not for her."

"So because it *wasn't time* for her, some young girl was raped and tortured, probably scared to death—" her voice faded away at the look on his face.

"No. She wasn't hurt. I don't know what happened. But

there—wasn't that tortured touch to her. I need to go. Are you coming?"

*Damned jerk*, Daisy thought a few minutes later as she drove over the rough roads. He sat next to her in silence. Hell, she couldn't even hear him breathing. *Spends so much time with his ghosts, he acts like one.*

It was unsettling. She couldn't hear him. He sat so still he could have been carved from marble—yet her senses were entirely too attuned to him.

He smelled good. Trapped in the close confines of the car, she was aware of just *how* good he smelled. Daisy had always been a sucker for the way a guy smelled. She didn't particularly care for cologne on a man, just the clean smell of soap and male.

And damn, this particular male was something else.

She was entirely too aware of him.

Being this close to him made her skin feel hot and itchy, made her aware of the way her clothes felt against her flesh, how her hair blew around her face in the breeze. Her heart started to slam against her ribcage and her breathing sped up. Against the steering wheel, she could feel her palms getting sweaty.

Up ahead, the gravel road ended and she had to turn off onto the dirt road. Eventually, that would end and there would be little more than two ruts in the dirt to follow and then they'd have to get out and walk the rest of the way to the field. She was looking forward to it, because she had to get out of this damned truck.

Then maybe she could think something else beside him.

Alone, in the middle of the night, with a man she didn't really know and there were murders being committed in her county, and the only thing that Daisy could really think about was how damned good he smelled.

Twenty minutes later, she had her wish.

Following behind him, she slammed her flashlight against her thigh and tried to figure how *this* had happened. "You know, I am the sheriff. I think I should be the one walking in front."

He didn't say anything.

Daisy slid her gaze back down the length of his back. And stared at his ass. Again.

Now she wasn't thinking about how good he smelled. For the past fifteen minutes, she had been trailing after him and in the bright patches of moonlight, she had been left to admire one very fine ass. "Any reason why you insist on being in front?" she asked irritably.

"Not sure where she is."

*Tanya.*

As they crossed into the clearing, she reached up to rub at her temple. "I'm still not entirely sure why we came out here. How can she help us? How can you even be sure you'll see..."

Something cold brushed against her. Daisy froze, jerking around, but she couldn't see anything.

Her eyes flew to Michael's face but he wasn't looking at her. He seemed to be staring at somebody just to Daisy's left, somebody roughly Daisy's height. His eyes were gentle, a soft smile on his face.

He didn't say a word.

*"Why is Daisy here?"*

Michael shrugged. He focused his thoughts, projecting them so that he didn't have to speak them aloud for them to be heard, *"She's the sheriff—if something's happened, shouldn't she know?"*

*"Why?"* Tanya's voice was flat and grim, her eyes angry. *"It's too late to do anything now."*

*"She's trying, Tanya. She can't turn back time. He isn't leaving any clues. She can only do much,"* Mike said, trying not to let her sense his frustration.

Tanya's eyes closed. *"I know. The girl's dead though. So am I. Can she stop him from doing it again?"* Her image wavered, a certain sign of rising emotion.

*"I don't know...that might be up to you."*

Tanya's eyes flew open. *"What can I do? Damn it, I'm stuck here. Here or at that damned cabin where he...where he..."* Her voice faded away and her eyes looked stricken as she stared at him, her image wavering in and out of sight.

*"Tell me who he is. Can you see him yet?"*

She spun away from him. *"No! I don't want to see him...he's just...just there! I can't—"*

Michael sighed. Running a hand through his hair, he glanced at Daisy. She was staring at him, her eyes wide and apprehensive. She'd sensed something from Tanya. Tanya had passed too close to her. The sheriff was a sensitive. She'd felt the cool touch of the deceased. He looked away from her pretty face and focused on

Tanya. *"It's okay—don't force it then."*

Looking at Daisy, he said, quietly, "Come on. Lets go for a drive." Maybe he'd get lucky and just feel something lingering from the young girl's passing. Daisy stared at him.

"We just went for a drive. *Here.* Now we're going for another one?" she demanded sarcastically. "What's with all the silent stares?"

Michael shook his head. "Nothing. There's nothing here right now."

"Nothing my butt," Daisy snorted, propping her hands on her hips. Arching one elegant brow at him, she said, "What's going on?"

Michael repeated, "Nothing." He walked between the two women, one living, one caught between the world and what waited beyond. The cool icy touch of death grazed his flesh as Tanya's arm brushed his. On the other side, he felt the warmth of life and the sweet scent of Daisy's body flooded his head.

*"Where are you going? I thought you came here to help."*

*"You're not ready to help me. I'll do it another way,"* he responded, trying unsuccessfully to block Daisy's scent from his head. She smelled too sweet.

"Where are you going?"

"We're leaving," he responded shortly. Too damned many voices in his head. "Nothing here right now."

"The hell there isn't. I felt something—damn it, you're the spookiest damned person I've ever met in my life. If you weren't talking to somebody then I'll eat my badge."

Michael stopped. Tanya circled around them, staring at him with shuttered eyes. "*You're supposed to help me—isn't that why you can see me? But you're just going to leave. Why aren't you helping?"*

*"I will help you—when it's time."* Turning away, he looked at Daisy. "Tanya's here. But she still can't help me. Can't help us. I'm sorry. There's nothing we can do until she's ready."

*"Stop talking about me like I'm not here,"* Tanya said angrily. *"What in the hell do you want from me?"*

Daisy stared at him warily, watching as he looked off to the left. Her eyes narrowed as she studied him. Her mouth parted and she whispered, "The diner…damn it, you were talking to somebody at the diner. Damn it, was there somebody you were talking to at the diner?"

Arching a brow, he asked levelly, "Did you *see* me talking to anybody at the diner?"

She scowled at him, her rosebud mouth puckering up as she replied snottily, "I didn't see you talking to anybody just now either, but I'd bet my next paycheck you were talking to somebody." She stood there, glaring at him in the moonlight with her hands fisted on her hips, her eyes glinting with temper.

And Michael suddenly had only one thing on his mind.

Kissing that scowl off her face.

Forget about the dead crying out for justice. Forget about the voices that had crowded his brain for far too long. Forget about the malevolent evil that darkened this small town.

He wanted to kiss her. It was the weirdest thing, too. Because Michael didn't forget about his responsibilities. He hadn't ever been able to silence the voices in his mind.

Her eyes flicked to his mouth and he heard her soft intake of breath. Taking a step, he heard a branch break under his foot. She spun away and he closed his eyes, muttering under his breath. *You've lost your mind.*

But another part of him said, *This is the closest to sane you've ever been.*

Turning away, he found himself staring at Tanya. Her gaze moved back and forth between him and Daisy, her pale, transparent features still full of fury. *"You're just going to leave? There has to be something else you can do. How can you just leave?"*

*"Because until you are ready to help me, there's nothing I can do here,"* Michael told her as gently as he could. Then he walked away.

After a minute, he heard Daisy falling in step behind him.

*You've lost your mind*, Daisy told herself.

Had he almost kissed her?

Had she almost kissed *him*?

And damn it, she was really disappointed when that kiss hadn't happened.

*Murder investigation*, hell-*O*! she shouted at herself. She really needed to sit herself down and have a talk, explain the basic rules of common sense. The weird guy passing through town wasn't the best guy to have a fling with—well, some people might argue he was the perfect guy for a fling. But Daisy didn't do flings. And if she did…well she just didn't. She was also a little busy trying to catch a serial killer before he killed one more woman. Definitely not the ideal time for any kind of romantic interlude.

*A couple hours of good, hard, mind-blowing sex might just clear your head and let you think better.* Okay, that was her libido talking.

She needed some sleep, that was what she needed. Well, sleep or a self-induced orgasm. Any of that might help a little. But instead of going home and telling tall, dark and strange here to get lost and come back when it was light out, they were out driving.

Stuck in a car with a man who did the weirdest things to her system. He made her skin buzz and at the same time, there was something about him that really, *really* freaked her out. He didn't talk, either. He just sat there, his hands resting on his thighs as he stared outside.

What in the hell he was looking at, she didn't know. Where they were going? She didn't know that either. At least earlier there was a destination. He'd been talking to Tanya in the field. She knew he had been. Now though, she wasn't so sure what his game plan was. Driving down 402 when it wasn't even three in the morning wasn't how she had planned to spend her night.

"I should have made some coffee," she muttered. She pressed her fingers against her eyes and rubbed, but it didn't make it any easier to hold her eyes open.

"He picked her up here."

Daisy hit the brakes. "What?" she demanded. Turning on the overhead light, she looked at him, feeling a cold chill dance up her spine. His eyes were glowing again.

"He picked her up here," he said quietly, staring off into the darkness. "She was hitchhiking. Wanted to go to Indianapolis—she'd never been. There was a play she wanted to see. Mom was afraid she'd get sick."

Daisy had absolutely no idea what to say. Swallowing, she shifted her gaze forward and realized she was still in the middle of the road. Easing the car to the shoulder, she shifted to park and turned the overhead light off. "Who is she? I can't do anything until I know she is."

He didn't hear a word she said. "She was walking—it was late, almost dark. She'd thought she'd get to town before it got dark. He pulled up and he just looked so safe…so normal."

Her palms were sweating. That icy cold sweat. Fear and rage clamored for equal footing inside her. Rage at whoever in the hell was doing this in her town. Fear that it was happening…and with such apparent ease…

And she was also uneasy as hell.

Michael O'Rourke was entirely too spooky. He didn't seem quite human. "Can you tell me something that will help me stop them?" she asked, her voice rough with emotion.

"She saw his face." He continued to stare out the window, but his voice seemed a little more focused, a little more there.

"You…you aren't talking to her, are you?"

He blinked and the glow faded from his eyes. A sad, but relieved smile curled his lips and he glanced at her. "No…no, she's gone. It's just—kind of like an echo."

"What's this about his face?" Daisy asked, closing her hands tightly around the steering wheel.

The smile that lit his face now wasn't sad, or relieved. It was downright mean. "She saw his face…I can't see him yet. But I'll know him."

Closing her eyes, Daisy thunked her head down on the steering wheel. "Damn it, shouldn't it be easier than this? Can't you just tell me who he is so I can go grab him?"

Michael started to laugh. "If you just go and grab him, even if I could tell you a name, you'd never be able to keep him. You're a cop, Daisy. Think like one. There has to be proof. He'll give himself away—when he does that, there's going to be proof."

Growling, she turned her head and glared at him. "Don't you think I've been looking for proof all this time? And while I wait, he'll grab another girl. If she died before he had his fun like you think, then he is going to be pissed."

Through the shadows, she could just barely see his face. The dim glow coming from the dashboard didn't give off much light. She watched as he leaned his head back against the seat and sighed. "I don't think he's going to grab another right now. He's not pissed—he's scared. Something has him scared."

# CHAPTER FOUR

Tanya hovered in the darkness, watching him. He had already methodically stripped the girl naked and right now, the clothes were burning away in the fireplace. Thanks to the gasoline he'd doused them in, there wouldn't be anything left of them but cinders and ashes.

Anger burned in the pit of her belly and frustration ate at her. Stuck here…stuck, trapped. Watching while he started to lift the still, pale body of the girl in his arms. Tanya didn't even know her name.

*"They'll find you—why are you wasting your time?"* When he jumped, it made her smile.

His hands were shaking as he pulled away from the girl and spun around. His eyes were wide and terrified as he searched the room. "Go *away*!" he rasped.

Tanya grinned evilly. *"I can't. You trapped me here. I can't leave until I do something."*

"Who in the fuck are you?" he screamed. His face was angry, florid and red.

She hadn't ever seen such emotion…Her heart stuttered in her chest as she found herself staring into his eyes. Nonononono…not him. Not him.

Her fury exploded through her and she didn't realize she had moved until he started to scream when she flew through the air. Wind started to whistle through the room.

*"Bastard!"* Her voice echoed through the room like a banshee's wail. She reached for him unconsciously and as she did, she saw his eyes move toward her hand and she realized he could see her.

*She* could see herself. Her hand was visible, pale and misty, transparent. But she could see it. Looking up, she met his eyes and knew that he saw her. Focusing the fury inside her, Tanya said to the man she had known all her life, *"You son of a bitch—I'm going to haunt you for as long as you live."*

He ran. Hard and fast. He was almost to town when reality settled in and he made himself slow down and suck his breath.

No. He hadn't seen her. She was dead. She screamed out his name, over and over, and then begged him to kill her. They always begged...his mind started to drift and a happy, dazed smile curled his lips as he remembered. The sound of their screams was such a sweet, erotic thrill.

Then a cold wind seemed to whisper over him and his smile faded. *I'm going to haunt you for as long as I live.* That voice, it wasn't like anything he'd ever heard, echoing around him, within him. She had come back. They didn't do that. They couldn't—damn it, this was all *wrong*. It was her fault. That little bitch. Fury and terror welled inside him and he wanted to lash out, but he didn't know how. His newest little toy was dead. She'd died before he could even have any fun with her. And damn it! She was still at the cabin—needed to get her out.

He started to turn and go back to get her.

*No.*

Memories of that face, that pale ghostly face rose in his mind and he knew he wouldn't go back. Not yet.

That face. Her eyes had been dark, too dark, like black pools in the pale circle of her face and she had screamed at him—it had sounded like death's war cry. He drove home, parking in the garage, but instead of climbing out, he just sat there for long moments.

"None of this is going right," he muttered, licking his lips. First that weird guy showed up in town. He didn't want changes. Changes weren't good right now. It hurt the status quo. Changes made the sheriff nervous and she was already nervous as hell—plus she started looking at odd things the minute he showed up.

Then the girl died.

Then the voices coming from the dark.

Now *her*.

A ghost.

He laughed hysterically. Ghosts weren't real, right? How in the world could ghosts be real? He shoved a hand through his hair and finally climbed out of the car. He edged around the car and made his way through the tight confines of the garage to the house.

It was dark inside and quiet. He needed the silence. He wanted to sleep, needed the quiet. He almost headed for the bedroom. A short nap, maybe a quick shower, and it would clear his head. He could think again and decide what he was going to do.

One glance at the clock though told him he didn't have the time.

Almost time for his shift to start.

ଔଓ

Michael came awake at the knock on the door.

His neck was stiff, his mouth was dry as cotton and his back hurt like hell after falling asleep at the desk. Slowly, he stood up and stretched, trying to ease the kinks in his muscles. It didn't do much good.

"Yeah?" He wasn't going to open that door until he knew it was the innkeeper. That woman made the Bureau look soft when it came to interrogation. Mike wasn't going through the inquisition again.

"It's Daisy."

The sound of her soft, husky voice started a low burn deep in his gut. His cock jerked a little and he pressed a hand against his fly. Just hearing her voice and he got hard. "Just a minute." He glanced at the computer. He'd bumped the mouse when he woke up and the images on the Bureau's website glared at him. He wasn't working this case in any official capacity, but he'd hoped there might be something in the Bureau's database that might help.

He'd been logged out due to inactivity but he didn't want the pretty sheriff seeing him there. If he had something to tell her, maybe. He didn't want her worrying that a lot more feds were going to show up, in an official capacity, and start poaching.

Mike had spent most of the night checking databases, hoping to find something. But no luck.

He padded over to the door and muffled a yawn. Shoving a hand through his hair, he opened the door. She looked a lot more awake than he felt, he thought tiredly. She held up a piece of paper but instead of looking at it, he just stared into her furious eyes. "She was fifteen. *Fifteen.*"

Michael felt yet another crack etch itself into his heart as he looked at the flyer. Kerri Etheridge. Fifteen. Runaway from Denton, Indiana. The bright red font across the bottom alerted authorities to the fact that she had a heart murmur.

"Heart attack," he said, closing his eyes. A blessing in disguise.

"You already knew that," Daisy said, her voice trembling with rage.

Michael glanced at her as he reached out and gently tugged the flyer from her. "I suspected it," he said, stepping to the side. She frowned at him but came in, crossing her arms over her chest. Turning around, she watched him while he closed the door.

*Kerri.* Pretty name. "She's worried about her mom." Michael closed his eyes. "She wants her mom to know what happened. She just wanted to go to a play." He crumpled the flyer in his fist, clenching his jaw. Impotent fury ate at him. He wanted to hit something. Anything. But instead of pounding on something with his fists, he dropped down onto the bed and stared at the crumpled flyer. "All she wanted to do was see a play."

"I can't say anything to her mom until I find her," Daisy said quietly. "Nobody has even seen her. If I say something now, without proof—that would be cruel, Michael."

"I know. Daisy, you don't seem to understand—I've been doing this a long time." *Too long…*

"You've been doing this *too* long."

His eyes flew up to meet hers and an unwitting smile curled his lips. He watched as she moved forward and knelt down in front of him. "This hurts you," she whispered, staring up at him. "I'm sorry. I wish I didn't need you to help me."

Michael reached out and traced his fingers along the curve of her cheek. "This is what I do, ma'am," he drawled. "Nothing to apologize about." Dropping his gaze to her mouth, he finally gave into the urge that had been driving him nuts ever since he'd seen her. Threading his hand through her hair, he drew her a little closer, slowly, giving her the chance to pull away.

Her mouth felt soft and she tasted like warm honey. He traced the seam of her lips with his tongue and her lips opened under his. With a groan, he eased off the edge of the bed and wrapped his arms around her, pressing his hands against her back. Her breasts flattened against his chest as he eased her up against him. Michael skimmed his fingers up her back so he could fist a hand in her hair. Pulling back, he scraped his teeth over the curve of her neck. "You taste good," he muttered huskily.

He could feel her heart slamming against his. She felt so damned alive—need fogged his brain and he couldn't think beyond anything but feeling that life, tasting it, bathing himself in it.

Reaching up, he grabbed the neckline of her shirt and jerked. Buttons popped and went flying. Shoving the edges of the shirt open, he stared down at the pale flesh of her breasts rising over the red silk cups of her bra.

He tumbled her down onto her back and buried his face against her breasts. The soft scents of vanilla and lavender lingered there and the warm, sweet scent filled his head.

"Michael…" Her voice was a soft hungry little whimper that made his blood burn even hotter.

The leather of her gun harness got in the way. With quick, impatient jerks of his hands, he unbuckled it and shoved it away before reaching below her to unfasten her bra. He tossed that aside and sat back on his heels to stare down at her. Her nipples were rosy pink—hard as ice.

His mouth watered and he hunkered down over her. Michael slid his hands under her and lifted her torso up to meet his mouth so that he could catch one plump nipple in his mouth. The other one, he caught with his thumb and forefinger, rolling it back and forth, pinching it lightly. She cried out sharply, her hands coming up to cup his shoulders. Her nails dug into his shoulders and she arched against him.

The heat of her was driving him mad. Everything about her felt warm, alive… Pulling back, he sucked air into starving lungs while he stared into her eyes. The soft golden-green eyes looked as hungry as he felt. "I want you," he muttered hoarsely. "So much I hurt with it. If you can't do this, tell me now, while I can still stop."

His eyes looked so damned tortured, Daisy thought. How in the hell had this happened? She'd come here because of a lost child—one she knew was dead. All she had was his word. She barely knew the man, but his eyes didn't lie. She'd come here because she had a job to do. How had she ended up half naked on the floor?

Daisy wasn't quite sure. But her belly was a hot, molten mass of need and she wanted him so bad, she hurt from it. She'd been too damned lonely for too damned long, and looking in his eyes did something to soothe that ache. Something that she couldn't even begin to describe.

She didn't need to, either.

Daisy didn't need excuses, reasons, anything. What she needed was him. Sleep hadn't done anything to ease the ache and the self-induced orgasm hadn't done a damn thing. This would.

Feeling his heat and strength against her while he pumped in and out, that would ease the ache. "I don't want you to stop," she murmured as she slid her arms up and wrapped them around his neck. Daisy drew him down against her, whimpering softly as the warm weight of his body crushed her into the floor.

He swore roughly and pulled away from her, crouching on his knees as he tore at her jeans. His hands were clumsy with need and there was a desperate look in his eyes. Kicking her tennis shoes away, she tried to help him but he just batted her hands away. Arching a brow at him, she rose on her elbows and smiled at him. "Demanding."

"Not usually," he mumbled. He slid her a look under his lashes and her mouth went dry. "I can't remember ever wanting a woman the way I want you, though."

Michael continued to hold her gaze with his as he stripped her jeans away, keeping the flat of his hands pressed against her thighs and just using the downward stroke of his hands to take the sturdy cloth down. She felt a hot flush rise to her cheeks as his eyes moved down, locking on her naked body with focused intent. "You're not wearing any underwear."

She smiled, shrugging a little. "Habit—I never wear panties with jeans."

A wolfish smile lit his features and his eyes once more met hers. She felt the heat from that look and it damned near singed her. It also hit her in the heart like a sucker punch—for once, that damnable grim look was gone from his face. "You shouldn't have told me that. I'll never be able to think straight around you again," he said, shaking his head slightly.

Flashing him a wide grin, she winked. "Oh, goodie…" Reaching down, she traced her fingers over his thigh. "You're overdressed, you know."

His lips brushed over hers. "Maybe I am." She watched as he rose and when he stepped away, she rolled over onto her belly to watch him as he walked across the room. Light filtered in through the gap in the curtains from the bathroom, but that was all. She'd like more light, wanted a room full of bright sunshine so she could sit down and stare at him at her leisure.

That body of his was amazing. His shoulders were wide and powerful, his chest tapering down into a flat belly and narrow hips. As he reached into the closet, she rose onto her elbow and admired the play of muscles in his back and arms. Hell, she knew women who loved to take trips into town and throw money away at strip joints. They were wasted—not one of them had a damn thing on Michael O'Rourke.

He wasn't doing a thing except rooting through a duffle bag, and he was wearing a worn out pair of jeans. When he pulled out a cellophane wrapped condom, she arched a brow and drawled, "I have to say, I'm damned glad to see you carry it in there, and not your wallet. I've never been impressed with men who carry them in their wallet."

Michael just looked at her, that small smile of his on his mouth. He crossed back to her and held out his hand, waiting for her to rise and take it.

She did and then her heart melted as he pulled her against him and just held her for a minute. *You're in trouble, Dasynda!* her brain screamed. *Big major trouble! He'll leave when his job here is done.*

She knew that. She also knew nothing had ever felt quite as right as his arms around her. Snuggling against him, she murmured, "You're still over dressed."

Daisy shivered as one big warm hand slid up her back, cupping the back of her head and then tangling in her hair before arching her head back. His mouth covered hers and she opened her lips, groaning as he kissed her deeply. He backed her up against the bed—she felt the edge of it against her legs just a moment before he urged her backward, covering her body with his.

He shifted his weight to keep from crushing her and she worked her hand between them, tugging at the button of his jeans, then easing the zipper down. She felt his groan as she slid her fingers inside his shorts, closing her fingers around him. He felt hard and smooth under her fingers, silk and steel. An ache pulsed through her womb and she rocked against him. Daisy managed to get in one quick, caressing stroke before he tore away and shoved his jeans down.

"You're hell on my mental state," he muttered shortly, glaring at her as he kicked his jeans away.

Daisy pushed up on her elbow, staring at him with a smile. Cellophane ripped and she watched him as he rolled the rubber down his cock before she looked at him with a wide grin. "You know, I think I'm actually probably really good on your mental state," she murmured.

Her grin faded away as he crushed her into the mattress. She sucked her breath as he pushed one knee between her legs, then wedged his hips between her thighs. Dark midnight eyes stared into hers as he pressed against her. Her lashes fluttered closed and he murmured, "No. Don't close your eyes—I want to see you."

Daisy felt exposed under that look. Foolish—she was naked in his arms, and he was pushing inside of her, but it was that watchful gaze that made her feel vulnerable. Too vulnerable, too exposed and she didn't like it. But she did want to see him. Dragging her lids back up, she stared at him as he slowly started to sink inside her.

The stretching sensation was unbearable. Catching her lower lip between her teeth, she arched up against him as he pushed inside her. He lowered his head, pressing a soothing kiss against her mouth. Skimming one hand down her side, he slid it under her hip, lifting her up against him.

Michael held her gaze with his as he pulled out. She sucked air in raggedly, trying to make her tense body relax. A lazy smile curved his mouth as he stretched out atop her, taking her hands in his, gently bringing them up by her head. The head of his cock was still inside her sex, throbbing, teasing the sensitive tissues there. He rotated his hips a little with his next stroke and Daisy gasped. He did it again and again, teasing her clit. "Shhhh…that's it," he muttered against her lips. "Relax."

Relax—hell, no. "I can't relax," she muttered. She arched up against him, taking too much in, too fast. She hissed and instinctively clenched her thighs.

Shifting against her, he cradled her head in his hands, lowering his head and taking her mouth. He also started to rock against her. Slow, gentle rolling motions that did little more than stroke his body against her clit. "Relax," he murmured again. He bit her lower lip gently and then sucked on it. One big hand gripped her hips, holding her still as he started to rotate his hips against her once more.

Heat built inside her like a volcano, escalating with each slow, teasing stroke. The pain eased a little more. Daisy wrapped her arms around his torso, raking her nails down his sides, arching against him, trying to rock her hips up and take him deeper inside. Michael just laughed softly, continuing those slow, gentle thrusts.

Little mini shocks started to quake in her belly, rippling through her sex. Daisy hooked her heels around him, trying to ride the thick ridge of flesh harder. As he sank just a little deeper, she moaned in satisfaction. A deep rumbling laugh escaped Michael and then he rose up on his hands.

The glittering look in his eyes was all the warning she had.

He took her thighs in his hands, draping them over his arms, then he started shafting her, hard, deep strokes. The bed started to shake beneath them. Daisy felt her heart slam into her throat as he rode her. Dear heaven, he was so damned deep—each stroke rocked her to the very core.

Staring up at him, eyes wide, she felt icy hot chills skittering all through her. Her skin felt too hot, too tight, too itchy. She couldn't breathe, couldn't see—the iron-hard thickness of his cock burned inside her, throbbing, aching. The rest of the world faded away and all she knew was his body moving over hers, his cock shuttling back and forth inside her sex. So hot, so deep, so tight.

*Too* hot. Too deep—too much, too much… "Stop," she gasped out, curling her hands over his shoulders. She pressed the heels of her hands against him but she wasn't sure if she wanted to push him away or pull him closer.

"Stop?" he whispered, sliding his hand over one sweat slicked thigh, cupping the curve of her rump in his hand. "Why?"

Staring blindly up at him, she said, "I can't…I can't…"

He just smiled. Lowering his head, he kissed her just below her ear and then he murmured, "You can." He reached between them and touched her clit. That one light touch did it. The orgasm ripped through her with an intensity that left her screaming breathlessly. And Michael continued to thrust inside her. Even as she came moaning back down to earth, he pumped inside, lowering his head to suckle on her nipples, first one and then the other.

"You still think you can't?" he whispered when she had her breath back.

"Huh?" she whimpered, staring up at him with blind eyes. Hunger and need left her uncomprehending. Her sex clutched greedily around his cock as he thrust against her. She clung to his arms, trying to make sense of his words.

He laughed, lowering his head to kiss her roughly.

Gathering her up against him, Michael buried his face against her neck. With short, deep thrusts, he rode her. Daisy rocked up to meet him, another climax building low in her belly even though she was still reeling from the first one. When he raked her neck with his teeth, she moaned raggedly. The brush of his fingers down her arm was like live electricity touching her skin.

The pounding of his hips against her grew more desperate—he shifted against her, slamming his hands down into the mattress by her head, rising up over her. With glittering eyes, Mike stared down at her, watching her so closely, staring at her so intently.

Daisy reached up, closing her hands over his biceps, digging her nails into the taut skin there as she lifted her hips up. The thick, steely flesh of his cock stroked over the sensitive, slick tissues of her sex—her heart slammed against her ribs while the heat built inside her, stretching her skin, threatening to spill out.

"Come for me," he whispered harshly, sliding his hand down her thigh and catching her knee, lifting it up over his hip. "Come for me, Daisy…"

As he pushed into her one more time, she did, clamping down around him and climaxing with a ragged scream. Her nails raked down his flesh, and she writhed under him, bucking in his arms.

He throbbed inside her—she felt the rhythmic jerking sensations of his cock. Moaning, her hands slid limply from his arms and he sank down against her, his head resting between her breasts.

Once she was able to breathe again, she whispered weakly, "How's your state of mind now?"

"I dunno," he murmured. "Maybe we should do that again and then see what happens."

"Again just might kill me," Daisy said, snickering.

"Ummm. Me, too. Hell of a way to go." Michael had to admit, he felt a hell of a lot better than he had been in a very long time. He could feel the furious pounding of her heart against his cheek, and the smell of hot woman filled his head.

The hot, snug silk of her sex still gloved his cock and he groaned as the tissues convulsed around him. "Gotta tell ya. I feel pretty damned good right now," he muttered. Sliding his hand up her side, he cupped her breast in his hand, rolling her nipple in his hand and watching it pucker.

She made a sound, that half moan, half laugh. "Don't do that—I'm practically dead already."

"I'm telling you—it wouldn't be a bad way to go." Her nipple was pink and tight and if he could just manage to move, he wanted to lick it again and taste her. Mike figured he could spend the next fifty years tasting her and he still wouldn't be satisfied. *Bad. This is bad.*

Daisy sighed. "I'd agree—but I've got a case to solve before I can think about dying."

"Yeah, you do. *We* do. She's mine—I have to help you finish this." He stared into her eyes and murmured, "I hope you understand."

A gentle smile curved her lips. "I do. And I have to tell you, I'm glad."

Working his arms around her, he rolled onto his back, bringing her with him. She sprawled on top of him and lifted up on her elbow, staring down at him. "This isn't the best way for you to spend your afternoon," he said. Her soft hazel eyes looked entirely too serious now.

She smiled a little. "Hey, I'm entitled to a lunch break." The smile faded. "I've got to find this girl, Michael. If we go around when I get off of work, do you think you might… Hell, how does it work?"

He reached up, pushing a silken lock of golden hair behind her ear. "Hard to explain that part. Kind of like a radio signal, sometimes. Best way to explain it. Sometimes I pick things up. Sometimes I don't. And yes. We can go whenever you're ready to."

She lifted a brow. "Ready? That will be exactly never. How can you be ready…" Daisy closed her eyes. "She was just a baby."

"I know. I wish I could make this easier. But nothing will." Michael held still as she lowered her head and pressed her lips to his.

"I *need* to do it now. But I'd have a hard time explaining it. I've got a meeting at one and five hundred other things I'm supposed to do before quitting time. Bureaucratic bullshit. I've got a killer to catch and I'm attending a committee meeting to discuss the need for a new stoplight."

"Hey, a town this small, isn't a new stoplight like a big step?" Mike teased.

It worked. A faint smile tipped up the corners of her mouth. "Yeah. A very big step." She sighed and cuddled against his chest. "You know, it's going to be a hell of a lot harder to concentrate on any of it now."

Ten minutes later, he watched as she climbed out of the shower, long streamers of dark brown hair dripping water down her sleek body. "Aren't you worried that people saw you come in here?" he asked, propping his shoulder against the door.

"I'm sure fifteen people saw me come in here. And I'm equally sure most of them have already called the majority of their friends and told them I'm here. So either you're my prime suspect, or we're having a torrid affair," Daisy said with a wry smile. "Either one is much more believable than the truth." Her voice broke off and she flashed him a wicked grin. "Well, I guess the torrid affair could be the truth now. But I can't exactly make it public knowledge that you're some sort of psychic bloodhound, can I?"

Michael ran his tongue along the surface of his teeth, watching as she started to dry off. "You aren't real big on beating around the bush, are you?"

She shrugged. "No. Wastes time." Slowly, she straightened, hooking the towel around her neck. "You know, I can't say I've had a lot of torrid affairs. Does one encounter count?"

Arching a brow at her, he said, "I'm not sure."

The blood drained out of his head, pooling in his groin as she moved up and pressed her nude body against him, wrapping her arms around him. "Well, I think maybe we might want to try for a repeat. If you're interested. That way, we can at least give truth to the torrid affair thing."

Chuckling, he trailed his fingers down her spine, he said, "Interested?" Nudging his cock against her belly, he asked, "What do you think? Am I interested?"

She hummed softly in her throat. "I think that's a yes."

# CHAPTER FIVE

The darkness had been hanging over his head all afternoon, like a damned cloud.

Ever since Daisy had left.

When the phone rang, he answered it with a short, "Yeah?" He knew he sounded pissed, but he couldn't help it. Even the sound of Daisy's voice didn't help.

"Hey. You okay?"

Michael tried to force himself to sound a little less distant as he responded, "Sorry, Daisy. Just feeling—odd. Are we ready?"

"Yes. I'm out front." Her voice was neutral, not quite mad, but…*cautious.*

Hell, he couldn't blame her. A few hours ago they'd been in bed together and he answered the phone sounding like a bear with a hangover. He couldn't help it, though. Something was wrong. It hung in the air, a storm waiting to break.

Grabbing his jacket, Michael started to head out of the room, but then he turned back. His bag was in the closet. His gun was in it. Slowly, he crossed over to it, taking the bag down and withdrawing the Glock and the holster. He slid the holster on and buckled it into place, staring stonily into the distance.

*"Things are getting ready to go down, brother."*

"I know that."

Lucas came walking into view, appearing out of the corner of his eye, his face blank. *"You don't like guns."*

"No, I don't. But I carry one when I have to."

*"The pretty sheriff the have-to this time?"* Lucas asked, leaning against the table. *"I got some vibes earlier."* He wagged his eyebrows and grinned.

Michael studied his brother with narrowed eyes. "You picking up eavesdropping?"

Lucas laughed. His image seemed to fade away for a minute and then he refocused, a little clearer, a little more solid. *"No, but damn, if I did, I wouldn't tell you. You'd just find a way to spoil my fun. It would be about the closest to living I've been in twenty years."* He shrugged, staring out the window as he added, *"I just know you, Mike. She's different—she means something to you."*

"Yes." That was all Mike would admit to. He didn't want to think about it, much less talk about it. The idea of caring about somebody was just too damn foreign to him. He'd given up on those kinds of emotions a long, long time ago.

*"You know who you're looking for?"*

Shaking his head, Michael methodically loaded his gun. That done, he slid the Glock into the holster and then pulled his jacket on. "No. If I did, you think I'd just be standing here?"

Michael lifted his eyes and stared at Lucas. "Do you know anything?"

Lucas smirked at Michael and said sardonically, *"If I did, do you think I'd just be standing here?"* The smile faded and his eyes closed.

Tension swelled in the room and Michael clenched one hand into a fist as Lucas wavered in and out of view for a moment. *"Things are changing around you, Michael. I don't understand what it is, not completely. But be careful—I made myself a promise and I can't move on until I see it done. Eternity is a long time to spend trapped here."*

Before Michael could form a single word, Lucas was gone. Snarling in frustration, he stalked out of the room. Ghosts—the most frustrating creatures on the damned planet.

They came, they went, they dropped ominous little comments like that and then before a person could ask so much as one damned question, they disappeared.

And Michael couldn't exactly stick a beeper on them, either.

Jogging down the steps, he slid silently out the door before Mrs. Maria Cambridge even saw him. No doubt she'd have fifty questions—she did every time she saw him. Michael would have loved to have stayed someplace else but Mitchell wasn't exactly a hotbed of tourism trade.

This small B&B was about all the town had to offer other than a hotel ten miles down the highway. And Michael's gut instinct had insisted he stay here. Crossing the sidewalk, he ducked into the car just as the door to the B&B opened behind him. He saw Daisy waving and he grinned.

"She's going to be so damned mad you slid past her again. She always manages to pin her guests down for interrogation…I mean friendly conversation, but you've evaded her entirely too well."

Michael shifted in the seat so that he could look at Daisy while he talked. "I doubt I have anything too interesting to tell her."

Daisy arched a brow, but remained silent.

"Okay, I don't have anything interesting I *would* tell her."

"Hmmm."

He didn't like the sound of that disinterested hum. Sighing, he ran a hand through his hair. Michael said softly, "I pissed you off, didn't I?"

She smiled brightly. "Why ever would you think that?"

Staring at her, he just waited. She pulled away from the curb, driving slowly down the busy street. People were leaving work, or coming into the small town for dinner at the diner. About as busy as this small place ever got.

She remained silent under his watchful gaze for long moments and then finally, hazel eyes slid his way. "I don't care to be brushed aside so quickly."

"You're talking about when I answered the phone just now," Michael said softly.

She didn't respond but the look in her eyes was answer enough.

"I wasn't brushing you off." Michael closed his eyes. "And I'm sorry if I made you think that." His gut started to churn and he didn't know if it was from the conversation's path, or something darker.

She slowed to a stop at the light and Michael could feel her watching him. He had to force the words out as he said, "There's just…something—"

Something cold brushed down his spine.

Turning his head, he found himself staring at a parked squad car. It was painted the same beige and browns as hundreds of other sheriff's deputies' cars throughout the country.

Nothing at all ominous about it. It sat parked in front of the bank, and Michael watched, unable to breathe, as a slender girl with short, spiky red hair came walking out. She passed by the deputy's car and paused to wave.

Michael couldn't see the man inside, but it didn't matter.

"That's him," he rasped hoarsely.

Blood seemed to flood his vision. Thick oozing red streams of it that poured across his line of sight like some bizarre Hollywood effect. Voices started to whisper. Then scream.

The voices of the dead had risen to banshee wails and it was sheer will that kept him from clapping his hands over his ears in an effort to drown the voices out. None of them made sense. There were no words, just those pain-filled, tortured cries, the mourning cries of those silenced far too soon, crying out for justice, begging for peace.

Even those who weren't trapped could suffer when their killer kept killing.

A hand came up, touching his arm. "Michael!"

Darkness swarmed up and flooded his vision—there was a roaring in his ears.

"Damn it, Michael, what in the hell is wrong?" The hand squeezed his arm, shaking him lightly.

He focused on that voice. *That* voice was alive. It was real. She was real. Sucking air in, he breathed in the scent of her. Vanilla. Wildflowers. Life. *Daisy*… Opening his eyes, he stared at her.

She was staring at him with turbulent eyes. "Damn it, what is wrong?" she demanded.

Her voice was too loud, rasping, grating on his nerves, but he seized on it, focusing on her voice, on the sound of her breathing. He forced himself to relax, made his lungs work again, forcing air in and out of his lungs, as he stared at her.

"If you don't answer me…"

Hoarsely, he said, "I'm okay—will be."

She blinked. "Damn it, you practically have a seizure on me and you tell me that you're going to be okay?"

Michael ran a shaking hand through his hair. He was sweating—covered all over with that nasty sweat that only came with fear. And rage churned in his gut. All the emotion pent up inside him made it damned hard to think, to focus on anything. "Sorry—hits like that sometimes."

Daisy stared at him. Shit. Her hand curled into a fist and she was tempted to just swing out and pop him on the end of that cleft chin. Instead, she took a deep breath and made herself pull to the side of the road, out of the flow of traffic as she muttered furiously to herself.

"Hits like that sometimes," she repeated, trying very hard not to growl. "You practically have a seizure. And all you have to say is *hits like that sometimes*."

Michael slid a look her way. His eyes were glowing. That had started just when he had gone stiff as a damned poker in the seat next to her, one hand flying up to the window, pressed flat. The other hand had briefly locked around hers, although she wondered if he remembered that at all.

He had arched up off the seat, his eyes rolling back, teeth bared. Never made a sound.

If his eyes hadn't been glowing that surreal shade of blue... As it was, that was the one thing that had kept her from calling for an ambulance. If an EMT had shown up and Michael stared at him with those glowing blue eyes, Daisy would have *more* trouble on her hands.

"Maybe you could have *warned* me about that," she snapped. Damn it, she was still scared to death. Turning sideways in the seat, she glared at him. "Now why don't you tell me exactly what it was that hit you?"

Michael wasn't looking at her though. He was staring past her shoulder, looking at something just beyond her. Or someone.

She turned, glancing behind her, but didn't see anything out of the ordinary. Just Mitchell on a Thursday night. "What?" she asked warily.

"It's him." There was no emotion on his face. None in his voice. Yet she sensed a rage so deep, part of her wanted to hide.

She turned again, trying to find who he was talking about. "Who?" she asked huskily, looking at the men walking by. She knew these men. Some she'd known since she was a baby—some she'd gone to school with. Hell, Marc Tanner, he'd been her first crush.

"The deputy."

# Chapter Six

She turned back to him with turbulent eyes. Shaking her head, she said flatly, "No."

Michael whispered, "He's stained with blood. I can't see him beyond the blood—I don't even know what he looks like."

"Look again!" Daisy said shakily. She reached for the handle to get out, but Michael leaned over and caught her arm.

"You don't want to believe me."

"You're damned right I don't!" she half screamed, trying to jerk away. "Damn it, that's *Jake.* He's like a brother to me. What in the hell do you know?"

Michael looked away from her face. Looking back at the deputy's car, he watched as the door opened slowly. He couldn't see the man though. It was like he had just been blotted away, his image replaced with a blood smear. "Because I look at him and see blood. Nothing but blood. And I hear their screams. Tanya haunts him. She won't leave him alone."

Daisy turned back around, and Michael could see the tears rolling down her cheeks as she stared at the deputy. Michael watched as the blood stained figure followed the woman from the bank. "She's next—he's been watching her for some time. He won't take her for awhile, but he dreams about it."

"Shut up," Daisy whispered harshly. "Damn it, just shut up." Dear God, she was going to be sick. She knew it. Not Jake. Damn it, he had been there when they had found two of the victims.

*Tanya.* He'd been there when they were looking for Tanya. Daisy moaned and pressed the back of her hand to her mouth, muffling the sound.

"I'm sorry."

Tears all but choked her. "If you are wrong about this…"

Michael sighed. "I'm not."

She looked at him. He felt his heart break as she stared at him with haunted eyes. "I know."

ꙮ

Jake owned a cabin a good thirty miles outside of town. Daisy sat at the computer in the county clerk's office, pulling up the files she needed. She did it with a blank mind. She couldn't think about what she was doing, or why.

If she did—if she did, she'd break. So she didn't think about it. She focused on the menial task, blocking out all other thought.

"What are you doing?" Michael asked.

He'd been very quiet, his voice neutral, almost as if he wasn't sure how to handle her right now. Hell, Daisy wasn't sure how to handle herself right now. She felt like she was going to shatter.

Slowly, focusing on each word, she said, "Looking for an address. Or an area. Jake…Jake owns a cabin." She flicked him a glance. "You said there was one."

Looking back at the screen, she continued to search through the files. Finally, she found the program she needed. "Damned clerks. Always updating things," she muttered. "They've changed the program they used to use."

She typed in Jake's information and waited. A few seconds later, the data scrolled on the screen. She printed the sheet out and stood up. Even though she couldn't hear him, she knew he was behind her. His quiet presence didn't set her on edge quite the same way it had before. It was almost like her system had adjusted to him—started trusting him on some very deep, very basic level.

She believed him. He was right about Jake. She knew it. The knowledge hit her like a fist in the belly. Tears burned in her eyes.

She really believed him.

Oh, dear God. Closing her eyes, she pressed the back of her hand to her mouth, trying to silence the tears rising inside her.

His fingers brushed against the back of her neck and she tore away, whispering harshly, "Don't. Okay? Just don't."

Clutching the address in her hand, she slid out of the room before he could say anything. Hell, what in the world could he say? He could try saying he was sorry, but what would that do?

It wouldn't make this any easier. Nothing would. Nothing ever could.

*One of my best friends is a killer.*

ঔ

*You can't…not right now.*

But he couldn't go back there alone. That bitch—her voice drove him crazy. And he *needed*…needed it. Hadn't had any fun with that last one—needed to feel that rush, needed to hear her scream again. Maybe, just maybe, it would ease the pain in his head, wash away the fog. Pain cleansed. Purified. Yes. It did.

He'd take her. Grab her. And when he made her scream, he would be able to think again.

*Her…*the faces all blended together. Their faces seemed to merge into one. The face shattered—reshifted. Formed.

Finally a face he could recognize. Somebody he could reach out, touch…take.

The voice of caution kept murmuring, *No, you can't, you can't…too soon, too soon.*

But he had to. He had to grab another one. Had to do something to shut up *that* voice. Had to shut her up. Or drown her out. The screams would drown out that voice. He knew it.

"Do it," he muttered. Swiping the back of his hand over the back of his mouth, he nodded. He watched as she pulled over, a satisfied smile on his face. Slow leak—imagine that.

Jake Morris turned on the flashers and parked behind Sandy Hampton. Casting a quick look around, he climbed out of the car and crossed over to her. "Hey, Sandy…what's the matter here?"

ঔ

Michael climbed out of the car, staring off into the woods.

They were parked in front of a dark quiet cabin. "Fishing rental. I've had to come out here a few times. People lose their keys, set the grill on fire…one woman locked her husband out because he'd spent five hours out on the lake and left her here alone."

He didn't say anything, tucking his hands into his pockets, as he looked off into the distance.

"We'll have to hike it from here. I'm not exactly sure where we are going. The lake is through this stand of trees. Jake's cabin is north of us, set back a little from the lake's edge." Daisy unlocked the trunk, digging out two flashlights and tossing one his way. "I'm not sure where. We're going to have to hunt for it."

He caught it automatically without ever looking her way. Softly, Michael said, "I can find it."

"You can find it," she repeated slowly. Daisy closed the trunk and turned to look at him. "How can you do that?" she asked quietly.

"I feel it. Let's go."

Michael smiled a little as he heard her disgusted sigh. But then, he lost track of her, of the night, of the trees. Everything faded away as the voices of the dead rose in the night around him. Not all of them had passed on. Some weren't strong enough—it took a lot of strength for a dead person's soul to be able to cross the veil that separated life and death. The trauma alone weakened them. But being here, this close to where their lives ended, Michael felt them.

The maelstrom of emotion pulled at him. His jaw clenched as he waded through it—like wading through waist-high mud. And the closer he got to his goal, the more his own anger grew.

There were a hell of a lot more than four victims. Mike felt the brush of so many souls that he lost count of them all. But there were dozens. He'd been killing for years.

Tanya felt him.

*"You found me…"*

Focusing his thought required too much effort. Out loud, he said quietly, "I told you I would."

Behind him, Daisy said, "Huh?"

He shook his head and continued to talk to the ghost. She hadn't fully manifested yet, but she had crossed over. Her own anger and pain had fueled it and soon, it would be too late. If he didn't help her move beyond this soon, she'd become one of the few things he did fear.

Poltergeists were the only ghosts that could cause harm. Their rage empowered them with a strength that was easily five times that of what they had in life. Guiding a poltergeist into the hereafter wasn't easy—Michael had done it before, but only twice. "I told you I would," he repeated, just as much to reassure himself as her. "We'll stop him."

*"You'd better hurry. There's another woman here. I can't watch this again, Michael. I can't—something is happening inside me. I don't know what it is, but I can't control it. Every time I look at him, I feel so angry, I don't even know myself."*

Behind him, Daisy asked quietly, "Michael…? Who are you talking to?"

"Tanya, don't you think you should be angry?" he asked as he jumped over a log. Turning, he held out a hand to Daisy only to find her staring at him with dark, troubled eyes.

"You're a spooky bastard, you know that, O'Rourke?" she said flatly even as she accepted his hand. She let him help her climb over the fallen tree that reached nearly to her waist. She dusted her hands off and muttered, "A very spooky bastard."

Slanting a grin at her, he turned back to the path and focused once more on Tanya. Nothing like trying to play a counselor to the deceased. She didn't need to try to suppress that rage—that didn't work. She had to let go of it if she wanted to move on. But they couldn't let it spiral out of control either.

*"Angry…yes, I have a right to be angry. But not at her…and I scared her. He came in with her—and I lost it. Now she's just as scared of me as he is. And what did she do? Nothing. The only thing she did was be stupid. We were both stupid…"* Tanya's voice and presence faded from his mind.

Michael stopped in the middle of the trail and tried to center his attention on what was around him, instead of what lay before him. Daisy stood behind him, her breathing soft and steady, but he could feel the tension rolling from her in waves. "We're close," he said quietly.

Daisy laughed—it was a high, wild sound. Her eyes were dark and terrified in the pale circle of her face, but he didn't once wonder if she would be able to handle this. "I figured that out while you were carrying on conversations with the dead. You couldn't have given me a warning about that, either?"

A bitter smile curled his lips and he looked at her. "My life is a little too weird for any warning label to cover it," he murmured. And that realization made him feel very, very bitter.

ᘓᘏᘐ

Adrenaline pulsed through him. Fear ate away at him, but he shoved it aside. He had to hear it, had to feel it—the screams weren't the same unless he felt her flesh. Until she struggled.

And it wasn't *right* when he was afraid.

He wouldn't be afraid once he touched her. His hands were clumsy as he went to work on her clothes and he hated it. He wasn't supposed to be afraid. It wasn't right.

At least *she* had finally shut up. Jake still couldn't believe that bitch had caused him this kind of trouble—haunting him. How could she haunt him? They'd grown up together…

A wild laugh escaped him as he cut away the soft pants that clung to Sandy's body. The sight of the cloth falling away calmed him inside. He could focus again.

The shaking in his hands eased and the roaring in his ears faded away, letting him focus on her fear. As he ran one palm down her thigh, pleasure spiked inside him. This was better. So much better.

He liked how she looked in them. They clung to her ass and thighs, then loosened, draping around her lower legs. She had such a pretty ass. He wanted to untie her ankles and turn her over, stare at her soft white curves, but he couldn't get careless right now. No—not now. Can't cut her loose—she'd wake up soon. Sandy had passed out, scared to death after *she* had been here. Wouldn't do for her to wake up and be half free.

Still, he slid his hands under her and cupped her ass, molding the soft, firm curves. Sandy moaned and Jake felt the anticipation roll through him. Blood pulsed hot and heavy through him, pooling in his groin. His penis felt thick and hard. Pushing up on his knees once more, he used his knife to cut away her panties.

Her lashes started to flutter open just as he reached for the button of his khakis. Lowering the zipper, he smiled at her, knowing that would be the first thing she saw.

"Jake…?"

He smiled. They were always confused at first. "Hi, Sandy." Covering her body with his, he kissed her.

She struggled to turn her head. "Jake—what are you doing?"

Fear started to crawl into her voice and he could see it when she started to remember. Her body tensed as she struggled, but the ropes only had so much give. He tied them so that she could move just enough, so that he could spread her thighs wide if he wanted. He usually preferred to keep their legs together when he mounted them. It was tighter that way. And he could feel them struggle better.

He donned a rubber before he covered her body with his. Ducking his head, he whispered into her ear, "Scream for me, Sandy."

A sob escaped her. "Damn it, Jake, what in the hell are you doing?"

ଓଃ

Daisy stared at the car with a heavy heart.

It was Jake's work truck. It was parked in front of the cabin and judging from the worn path, Jake came out here on a fairly regular basis. She didn't want to think about what he did out here.

The windows were covered with thick wooden shutters, but she could see light seeping under them. A perfect place for a crime—they were far away from the nearest neighbor. Sound would carry on the water, but his cabin was far enough back from the lake that it would dampen the sound. Far enough back that it wouldn't be seen. The shutters would silence even more sound.

"You bastard," she whispered, starting to move past Michael.

He caught her arm, trying to push her behind him. That was when she saw the gun. Narrowing her eyes, she whispered, "I really hope you have a license for that."

Michael just cocked a brow at her.

Of course he had a license. He was a fucking FBI agent. So what if he didn't exactly look like one. Daisy hissed out a breath. Still, this wasn't his job. It was hers. The women Jake had killed, they were hers. He started forward and she grabbed his arm, jerking on him. His eyes met hers and she shook her head furiously.

He glared at her.

Daisy just glared back and then she shoved in front of him,

drawing her gun and holding it in a loose grip by her thigh. She heard him sigh behind her and she grinned. Nice to be the one frustrating somebody for a change.

She could hear voices now, muffled, too indistinct to really make out. The walls were soundproofed or something. Daisy ought to be able to hear him better than this. Done to keep anybody from hearing the screams. Damn it. They were on a slippery slope here and she knew it. Jake had a woman in there, one he was planning to kill and Daisy had absolutely no legal reason for being out there.

Somehow, she didn't think it would fly if she explained to a judge and jury that the reason she arrested Jake was because a psychic had told her that Jake was a killer. Going on the word of a psychic who worked for the FBI might sound cool, but it wouldn't hold up in court. Hell, it wasn't enough for a search warrant.

She'd had a vague plan, finding some kind of evidence to implicate him, plant it if she had to, something, anything, whatever it took to stop him.

Instead, she had a killer on her hands, no reason for being here, and hell, yes, she could arrest him, but other than assault—all those thoughts cluttered her mind as she drew closer to the front door.

*Get her out of there now—details later…*

Just barely she could hear a soft male laugh. A woman's terrified cry. "…what in the hell are you doing…"

She stepped back but before she could even look at him, Michael had guessed what she wanted. He busted the solid wooden door down with one swift kick and stepped inside. Daisy followed, her gun focused on Jake's head. "Yeah, Jake," she said flatly. "What in the hell are you doing?"

He lay sprawled atop Sandy's pinned body, his khakis shoved low, the rest of him clothed. He rolled away from her, jerking his pants up, and Daisy saw him grab the gun on the table by the cot.

"Put it down, Jake."

He laughed as he crouched on the floor behind the cot, keeping Sandy's pinned, terrified body between them. "Hello, Daisy." Something black and ugly filled his eyes as he looked at Michael. "I don't think I will put it down. You need to put yours down, though. Otherwise…"

Nausea churned in her gut as Jake lowered his head and pressed his lips to Sandy's brow. Then he replaced his lips with the gun's muzzle. The cold, matte black metal pressed into soft white flesh and Daisy could see Sandy's flesh give way as Jake dug in. "*You* put your gun down, Daisy. Otherwise…she won't leave here alive."

Daisy shook her head. "You're talking to another cop here, Jake."

Jake barked out a laugh. "A cop? Hell, I'm a second rate deputy in a second rate town, playing Barney to your Andy. Stuck here in Mayberry, practically. I don't see myself as the next shoo-in for *Law & Order*."

He cocked his head, trailing the fingers of his other hand along Sandy's body. She whimpered, cringing away from his touch, turning her head and staring at Daisy with wide, terrified eyes. "Now, put the gun down—both of you."

A soft chuckle drifted through the room.

Daisy shivered at the sound. That wasn't Michael—and by the look on Jake's face, it wasn't him either. It was soft, feminine and scary as hell. When the voice came, it took everything she had in her to keep from dropping the gun and flinging herself at Michael in terror.

*"Guns…why are you so worried about guns? That's not what killed me."*

Jake shoved away from the cot, staring around the cabin. His eyes were wide, almost black in his suddenly pale face. "Go *away*."

*"I will. When I know you're burning in hell."*

An unseen wind started to whip through the room, tearing at Daisy's clothes. She squinted her eyes against it, watching Jake. She ducked to the floor as he started to wave his gun around through the air. From the corner of her eye, she could see Michael doing the same.

"Tanya, don't scare him so bad that he starts shooting at thin air," Michael said.

With a desperate laugh, Daisy echoed, "Please, Tanya." *Now, I'm talking to a dead woman…* "I'd rather get her out of here in one piece, and me as well. And I'd like to make sure he can't do this to anybody else."

A soft sound echoed around them. Like a sigh. *"Don't worry. He won't. He won't hurt anybody. Ever."*

"Make her go away!" Jake screeched, turning his head to stare at them with wild eyes. He grabbed Sandy, fisting his hand in her hair.

He pressed the gun to her cheek, hard. "Make her go away or I'll kill this bitch and give her company."

Daisy stood slowly, shaking her head. "Don't do that, Jake.

Come on—leave Sandy alone. This isn't her fault."

"No. It's *her* fault." He glanced up at the ceiling again. Unable to keep from looking, Daisy followed the path his eyes took. And there she saw her. A pale white figure just hovering there.

The wind blew faster and harder. It got colder. And the colder it got, the clearer that figure became. *"My fault. My fault—you bastard..."* Tanya started to laugh. She moved closer, a mean smile on her mouth. *"You're the one afraid now, aren't you?"*

Drifting down from the ceiling, she started to circle around Jake and he flinched, letting go of Sandy and scuttling away. He cowered in the corner as the misty white form moved closer.

"Nonononononono!" he screamed harshly, swinging out with one hand. It seemed like he had forgotten he was even holding the gun, just slapping out blindly in terror.

*"I screamed that, didn't I? How often did I beg for help? Beg you to stop? You laughed. You wanted me to scream—now it's my turn."* Tanya's voice rose and fell, getting louder and louder until it echoed off the walls.

Michael sat there, listening to that terrifying voice with dread. She continued to taunt her killer, her voice low and full of hate. The rage and anger spiraling inside her. It flooded the small confines of the cabin. All that emotion was going to explode and the results were going to be ugly and scary as hell.

She was pulling herself back into this world, too completely. Too entirely. Leaning over, he put his mouth to Daisy's ear. "Get the girl loose. Got a knife?"

Daisy gave a slight nod and started to inch away, moving backward until she could press her back to the wall. Once there, she circled around the room, watching Jake carefully. Jake never once looked her way. He was too focused on Tanya. Nobody else in the world mattered to him.

Michael waited until he saw Daisy kneel by Sandy's side before he spoke to Tanya. "Is he worth it?"

Tanya barely seemed to realize he was talking to her. She was too busy whirling around Jake, her laughter high, a wicked edge to it that made his skin crawl. *"Scream for me!"* And her voice sounded just a little more solid. Long plumes of misty white trailed from her as she tormented him, making her seem larger than she really was.

Michael focused—it was harder now than ever before. All that wild manic energy that she drew in with her was scrambling his brain. "*Tanya!*"

The whirling white form seemed to settle a little and she turned, staring at Michael. *"Go away now,"* she said quietly.

Shaking his head, Michael said, "I can't. You said you could feel something odd, something inside you changing. Rage is taking a hold of you, Tanya. Ghosts and rage don't mix well. Ghosts and rage—you let rage settle inside you, Tanya, you'll never move on. Being stuck here, is that what you want?"

She stilled. *"I want him to pay."* Hatred filled her eyes and she stared at Jake malevolently. *"I want him scared and begging for his life."*

Tanya looked back at Jake and Michael cursed under his breath as she started to scream at Jake again. She reached out, her arms long, much longer than a human's, and grabbed him. Michael dove across the floor as she flung Jake across the room. "This makes him pay—but you pay as well. Don't punish yourself for his crimes. You don't want to be trapped, Tanya. Let it go. I'll take care of him."

*"I…I don't think I can do that."*

Michael closed his eyes as her anger began to pulse within him—getting too strong. Too out of control. "Are you ready to make us suffer with him?"

Daisy crouched in the corner with Sandy huddled against her. There had been an old, rough blanket laying on the floor and Daisy had given it to the younger woman, but Sandy was still trembling. Soft little mewls of fear kept rising in her throat and she stared sightlessly at the wall. Her entire body was shaking,

She was going into shock. Daisy had to get her out of there but she didn't know how. She sure as hell couldn't carry Sandy back to the car. It had been a good mile hike to get here and a rough one, at that.

It didn't help that the very air around them felt heavy, icy with terror. It was like the way the air felt thick and humid right before a summer storm broke open right over your head, but instead of thick, muggy air, when Daisy breathed in, it was chills and fear that clogged her lungs.

Closing her eyes helped a little. Forcing her breathing to level while she counted to ten. No—twenty. Twenty was a little better. She'd prefer a thousand, but she really needed to figure a way out of this mess.

Her mind raced. This sure as hell hadn't been covered in training years ago, and it wasn't anything she'd ever picked up through experience either. Part of her knew she needed to get Sandy someplace safe, someplace where she could get medical treatment.

The other part didn't want to do a damn thing that would draw Tanya's attention away from Michael. And yeah, she wanted to hear more about this *us suffering with him* part.

*"I won't hurt anybody else—just him."* Tanya's voice was low and angry and there was a sadistic look in her eyes that made Daisy's skin crawl.

Michael cocked his head, staring at the incorporeal form as though he was talking to somebody on the street about the damned weather. "But you already have—you scared her earlier, didn't you? You already told me that. You can keep it to where only he can hear you, but you're losing control. The anger is taking control."

Chills ran down Daisy's spine as she watched the emotions that flickered on Tanya's face. She seemed to getting more and more *solid* with every passing moment. That really *really* bothered Daisy—because she also sensed a wariness about Michael. Not in the way he held himself, or even the way he talked.

She doubted that Tanya sensed it at all.

But he was worried. Very worried.

"Listen to me, Tanya. If that anger takes over completely—if you let go, you'll lose yourself. And passing on, you will never be able to do it. You'll be trapped here, nothing more than a thing of anger and rage that nothing short of God's intervention will stop. I won't be able to help you."

Okay, now *that* sounded bad. Images of the movie *The Grudge* began to roll through Daisy's mind. Before she realized she was going to say anything, she heard herself speak, "He's not worth that, Tanya. Anger wasn't something you had use for in life. Remember how I always held grudges? You never did. Said you were too lazy, but it wasn't that. You just didn't have any use for anger. Not then. Don't let it take over now."

Seconds later, it was like the storm just rolled away. The terror was gone. Daisy was no longer trembling and Sandy finally stopped whimpering in mindless terror. Daisy squeezed Sandy's shoulder and then looked to Tanya.

Or tried to—Tanya wasn't so easy to see any more.

*"You always had the most annoying habit of being right, Daisy,"* Tanya said. Her voice sounded distant, like it was coming from down a well. The wind whipping through the cabin stopped—there was a soft sighing sound and then just silence.

"Tanya?"

Michael glanced at her. "She's gone."

Daisy gaped at him. "That fast?"

That crooked grin appeared for the briefest second. "Sometimes, it just takes the right words. You had them. I didn't." Then he blinked. As he looked away, she had the briefest glimpse of his eyes. That look was going to stick with her a long, long time.

"I have to take him in, Michael. And we have to hurry. She's going into shock."

Michael looked away from Jake for a moment. Jake was still huddled on the floor, his arms over his head. Of the four of them, Jake still seemed to be suffering the after-effects of whatever Tanya had been doing. He was bawling like a baby. A disgusted sneer curled Michael's mouth and then he looked at Daisy. "Prison's too good for him."

As he moved toward Sandy, Daisy thought that danger had been averted.

Obviously not.

"She'll sleep now," Michael said less than a minute later as Daisy was slowly, carefully approaching Jake.

Daisy looked back at Sandy. "Damn it, shock victims aren't supposed to sleep!"

His eyes met hers very briefly. "She's not in shock any more."

Daisy tried to block him from Jake, but he merely moved around her with that easy, effortless grace, crouching in front of the fallen man. He watched Jake for the longest time with that piercing, glowing gaze. "Tanya's gone."

Jake yelped at her name and looked up. Whatever he saw on Michael's face didn't set him at ease. He cringed away. Daisy suspected if he could have disappeared into the wall, that's exactly what he would have done. "Get away from me," he whimpered, sounding more like a child than a grown man.

Michael nodded. "I will. They want you more than I do anyway."

"They…?" Jake whispered timidly, his eyes wheeling around the room.

Daisy glanced around, too. Holy hell. Please, not more. She couldn't handle anything else weird tonight. Maybe never. She might be ruined for ghost flicks for life. But there was nothing else in the room. Nobody else. Just the four of them.

She looked back to the two men in time to see Michael reaching out. He held nothing in his hand, yet Jake screeched in terror. "No! Don't fucking touch me!"

Michael did, though. Something odd happened when he touched his fingers to Jake's temple. There was a glow—a faint echo of the blue glow she saw in Michael's eyes. And for the briefest second, Jake's dark brown eyes glowed blue.

A keening wail escaped the deputy. He buried his face in his arms. "No—make them stop. Don't…take it away, please please please!"

Michael stood up, turning his back on Jake without a word.

Daisy continued to stare at Jake with wide eyes, watching as he slowly started to rise, batting at thin air. His eyes were desperately searching the air for something, and he kept shouting out, screaming at something that Daisy couldn't see.

"What did you do?"

Michael's face was weary. "Giving the rest of them peace. They just want to know why." He stopped in his tracks, staring at her.

Daisy shook her head. "But there isn't a why. Men can't always explain why they kill," she said softly, watching as Jake continued to spin around, staring into the air and swinging his arms as though he was trying to fend something, or someone, off. "Are…are they all trapped?"

"No. Just—at unrest. Most of them have moved on, but they can still see him, feel him. Each time he kills, it leaves a mark on them. When he's gone—"

Daisy shook her head. "Gone? No. No gone. He's going to prison."

Michael looked at her, a sad smile on his face.

"What?" she demanded. "What do you know?"

"They won't let him live that long."

Before she could puzzle that one out, Jake took off running. At some point, he'd dropped his gun and Daisy breathed out a sigh of relief as she went after him. Chasing somebody with a gun was something she'd planned on leaving behind her when she left

Louisville Metro.

Jake ran east, heading for the lake. She hit the button on the flashlight and followed after him. Branches slapped at her face, tangled in her hair and she could feel leaves, twigs and mud sliding under her boots as she ran. "Just let me stay on my feet," she prayed silently.

The path curved and she struggled to close the distance between her and Jake before he got around the bend. She lost sight of him, though as the path continued to weave in and out of the trees. Blood pounded in her ears and her heart was racing so fast that she couldn't hear anything else.

"Damn it, where in the hell are you?" she muttered.

"Am I wasting my breath if I tell you that you don't need to chase him?"

Hell. She hadn't even heard Michael leave the cabin. Slowing to a stop, she stared ahead. "Go back and stay with Sandy. And yes, you'd be wasting your breath. Get Sandy to the car—I assume you know how to use a radio. Call for back up."

Michael sighed and she felt his hand brush down her hair. "You'll find him in the lake. I'll wait until I hear from you to call for back up."

Spinning around, she glared at his retreating back. "Damn it, I said…"

Distantly, she heard a splash. Sound carried on the water. And the lake was close now. A few hundred feet away. That was a big splash, too. Turning back to the trail, she started to jog, and then run. The trees broke open around her and she made her way to the dock, shining the flashlight around warily. Jake was nowhere to be seen. "Wait until you hear from me to call for back up," she muttered, shaking her head. Damn his stubborn hide.

An owl hooted and Daisy jumped.

"Oh screw this," she said furiously. She'd go back and call for back up.

But even as she turned, her flashlight flickered off the lake, reflecting light back at her. Michael's words echoed through her mind. *You'll find him in the lake.*

In the lake. Daisy swallowed. Not on the lake. Not by the lake. In the lake. Dragging her tongue over dry lips, she walked over the weathered boards of the dock. The heels of her boots echoed hollowly with every step. A fish jumped somewhere and the splash made her jump yet again. "I swear, I'm sleeping with the lights on every night for a month," she breathed softly as she edged closer, shining the flashlight's beam out over the surface of the water. Jake wouldn't try to swim to the other side at night, would he? Easier to get away just by making his way around the lake's shore. Hell of a lot safer, too.

She reached the edge of the dock and scowled. "Damn it." She let the light fall to her side but as it did, it shone on a pale face. Eyes wide. A hideous death mask.

Daisy screamed. Clapping a hand over her mouth, she stared down into the water at Jake's still face. "Oh, dear God," she whispered quietly.

It hadn't even been ten minutes since he had taken off running from the cabin. Maybe four minutes since she had heard the splash.

And now—

*They won't let him live that long.*

# CHAPTER SEVEN

It was late the following night when she finished the official report.

*Officially,* Jake Morris' death was an accident. He'd tried to run when Daisy attempted to arrest him. Why was she out there? A wonderful standby—an anonymous tip. And since Jake wasn't around to lawyer up and have her worry too much about him getting out of prison on technicalities, she felt safe using it.

Officially, the report looked very cut and dry. Probably one of the neatest little wrap up jobs on a major case in history. No question of his guilt, not with everything they'd found in the cabin and no need to worry about him getting off on some technicality at the trial. All nice and tidy with no loose ends.

Unofficially—it was the most bizarre night of her life. The most terrifying. One that was going to be the source of nightmares for some time, she had no doubt. It was definitely one that she hoped never to repeat again.

Yet as she finished printing the report out, she couldn't help feel a little bitter.

Michael was going to leave.

He had stayed here only because there was a ghost who couldn't move on. And now that Tanya had moved on, he would, too.

A few days. A handful of days, she'd known that man. She didn't know much of anything about him, other than the fact that he had the saddest blue eyes, a smile that melted her knees—and he was too damn spooky to describe. But she desperately wanted him to stay. There were men in this town she'd known off and on all her life and she wouldn't miss any of them if she up and decided to move back to Louisville. Not that it would happen, but Michael, she was going to miss him. She already did.

How had he come to mean so much in such a short amount of time?

Sighing, she propped her elbows on the desk, rubbing at her eyes with her fingers. Chances are, he was already gone. They'd spoken briefly at the hospital. Michael had told her that Sandy wouldn't remember a lot of what had happened. Vague memories of Jake grabbing her, and nothing else.

She was rather curious about that, but he'd just given her that small, mysterious smile of his. And that was all the answer she would get. Daisy could fill in the blanks though. If he could make Sandy sleep, do something to keep her from going into shock—wiping a few memories away was probably just another talent.

A part of her cringed at the thought. Memories were personal—should Sandy's have been touched? But every time Daisy closed her eyes, she remembered what happened at the cabin. Sandy would have enough bad memories just from Jake grabbing her, just thinking about what *might* have happened. She didn't need memories of ghosts on top of it.

"You should be at home. You're exhausted."

Daisy jumped. Looking up at Michael, she slammed her hand down on the table and snapped, "Don't do that!"

His eyes softened. "I'm sorry." He closed the door behind him and leaned back against it, studying her. "Were you able to sleep any today?"

Daisy shook her head. "No. I'll sleep tonight. Maybe. Then again, it may be a few days before I can sleep." She paused, looking down at the report in front of her. It was done. All she had to do was sign it. "Almost done here." A knot formed in her throat as she saw the bag over his shoulder. "You're leaving."

The thick fringe of his lashes drooped, shielding his eyes. "My job here is done," he said quietly, lifting his shoulder restlessly.

He looked back at her, his gaze resting on her mouth for a brief second. Then he met her gaze and forced a smile. "So it's time to go."

It wasn't the first time Daisy had thought about it, but now, she looked at him and wondered, really wondered, just how deep the loneliness inside him ran. "You ever get tired of just the job, Michael?" she asked softly.

"It's all there is for me."

Slowly, Daisy rose from her desk, moving around it. She held his gaze as she drew nearer and hoped the knot in her throat wasn't going to choke her before she could finish saying goodbye. "Is it that way because you want it to be? Or because you don't think you can have anything else?"

He had no answer. Daisy forced a smile. "Maybe you don't know. Think about it." Rising on her toes, she pressed her lips to his mouth gently. "When you know—I'd be interested in hearing the answer. Because if you think it's the second one, I'd like the chance to prove you wrong."

She started to pull away and his hands came up, cupping the back of her neck and pulling her closer. His tongue traced the outline of her lips and then pushed inside. Desperate goodbye sex was so…desperate, but Daisy couldn't pull away.

She slid her hands under his shirt, feeling the smooth play of hard muscle under his skin. He felt so warm, strong—so alive. It was weird. Daisy hadn't realized it until just that moment, but she hadn't felt this alive for a long, long time. When he left, it was going to leave a hole inside her and that life would drain away, leaving her empty.

But she wasn't going to ask him to stay. If that was what he wanted, he'd do it. If he was going to leave, Daisy wanted one more memory with him. She rose up against him and he wrapped his arms around her, lifting her off the floor. "You taste so good," he muttered.

"Mmmm. So do you." She could feel tears burning her eyes but she wasn't going to cry.

She left then, walking away from him before he could see the tears gleaming in her eyes.

❧

*"Don't do this, Mike."*

The long endless stretch of highway unfurled beneath him as Michael headed out of Mitchell.

And riding shotgun with him was his brother. Sighing, he glanced at Lucas. "Don't do what?"

*"Don't just walk away from her."*

His gut knotted even thinking about it. He didn't want to walk away. He wanted to turn the car around and go back to her, wrap his arms around her and hold her until she got some rest. Then he wanted to kiss her awake and make love to her, long and slow.

But it wasn't going to happen. Right now, he was functioning on sheer instinct. Case solved, job done, drive away, find some quiet place, and rest. That was what he needed—what he tried to do any time he did a job.

*"This wasn't a damned job! You aren't on the payroll for this."*

Michael snorted. "The agency doesn't just pick and choose where I'm going to go, Lucas. I go, and just end up in places like this. That's how my life works." Bitterly, he muttered, "This is all there is."

*"Just because it always has, does that mean it has to stay that way? You have a choice—a chance at a real life. Reach for it."* Lucas shook his head. *"Don't do this, Mikey. She's your chance."*

"I can't."

*"Why?"* Lucas demanded. Anger surged through him and his form went from damn near invisible to almost solid as he glared at Michael. "*After all this time, don't you deserve it?*"

That, Michael didn't know. "I don't know." Then he shook his head. Yeah, he did. He knew all right. He *didn't* deserve any kind of normal life. Even if he did, he couldn't have it. "I don't have a normal life—I wouldn't know what it was like if it bit me on the ass. But I don't deserve it, Lucas."

*"Why not? Over me? Let it go, Mikey. You were twelve years old, damn it. You can't keep punishing yourself for not protecting me. I was the big brother—it was my job to protect you, not the other way around."* Lucas shook his head and said, *"Let it go, Michael. Give up your ghosts."*

Now Michael laughed. "That's impossible. The door's been opened—I can't close it."

Lucas smiled sadly. *"You don't have to. Just…stop hunting for us. If somebody needs you, they'll find you. Tanya did. You may never have a completely normal life. I get that. But you can have a happy one. If you'll reach for it."*

Daisy's image bloomed in his mind's eye. Groaning, he slowed down and edged his car to the side of the road.

A happy life—not something he'd ever really thought much about. He didn't know if he was in love with her. Michael wasn't certain he really even understood love. But she was the first woman he'd ever met that made him wonder about it. Sex was easy. Love, though—he wasn't so certain about that. Yeah, she made him wonder, made him yearn and wish. Made him want.

*I'd like the chance to prove you wrong…*

A smile appeared on his face. She could do it. If anybody could, it was her. There had been a few brief moments with her when he hadn't thought about the ghosts, when he hadn't thought about Lucas, when he hadn't thought about anything but her. "I barely know her," Michael said softly.

"*Then get to know her. Isn't that what dating is for?*"

Leaning his head back, Michael chuckled. "Dating." He spent his life talking to ghosts and hunting down their killers. Dating seemed just a little too—tame.

"*It's called real life, Mike. Reach for it.*"

ଔଓ

The lady was so damned tired, not even Sarah's warning bark woke her up. She hadn't even fed Sarah when she came home. She'd stripped off her clothes as she walked to the bed and fell face down. It had been daylight then and now it was black and still the lady slept.

The retriever watched the door with wide, liquid eyes as the doorknob jiggled. Tumblers rolled. It unlocked and moments later, the deadbolt followed suit. It swung open to reveal a man. He paused by the dog, tucking something inside his jacket, before crouching down in front of her.

Sarah could smell her lady on him.

"I'm no threat," he murmured.

*Deep voice…nice voice…*Sarah leaned into his hand as he scratched behind her ears. *Ooooohhhh…nice hands.*

He chuckled. "I think you know that."

When he headed down the hallway, Sarah followed behind curiously. She'd hoped maybe he would get her some food, but he couldn't look away from the lady. He stood in the doorway for a minute, just staring at her. Sarah finally went and curled up below the window.

People never made any sense to her. She could tell what he wanted just by the way he smelled. And all he did was stand there.

She was sound asleep. Michael hadn't sensed anybody awake inside the house as he climbed from his truck. Well, other than the dog. He'd have to talk with Daisy about that dog, too. He knew he had a way with animals, but that dog was entirely too friendly, too trusting.

Leaning his shoulder against the doorjamb, he just stared at her. Moonlight shone in through the window, painting her skin with a soft, silvery glow, turning her hair to a pale blonde. In sleep, she looked so soft and delicate. She was an Amazon, though. She had the heart of a warrior. What had happened at the cabin would have had most people running for the hills, but instead of running, instead of breaking down and crying, she had stood up and faced down a poltergeist. Tanya's rage had been increasing with every breath. Mike's blood had long since gone cold with fear.

But Daisy had stood up and faced Tanya. Brought her back from the very brink.

He didn't think he'd ever met anyone with that kind of strength.

He wanted to climb in bed and cuddle up behind her, just wrap his arms around her while she slept. For a few minutes, he stood there, waiting to see if she'd wake up. Michael almost left. Almost… He slowly slid out of his jacket, draping it over the foot of the bed. Then his boots. He left the rest of his clothes on. She wasn't wearing much of anything, he could tell. If he climbed in bed with her naked—well, he was already going to have some explaining to do.

Stretching out on top of the covers, he pressed up against her back, sliding his arm around her waist. Daisy sighed, snuggling back against him. Michael smothered a groan as the soft curves of her ass pressed against his hips. The blood in his veins re-routed and all headed south, leaving him questioning his sanity.

His cock ached. Unable to help himself, he arched his hips and pressed just a little tighter against her.

Daisy sighed in her sleep. "Michael…" Then she shifted a little, wrapping her arm so that she could lay her hand atop his. A satisfied little hum escaped her and then she was still.

Behind her, Michael lay staring into the darkness. The sound of his name on her lips as she slept was a memory he was going to carry with him for a very long time. It was hours before he slept. But he didn't give a damn. Even though he ached with weariness, he was content to just lie there, holding her.

ꕥ

Heat.

Daisy groaned, trying to struggle out from under the covers. Although why in the hell…

Her hand pressed against warm male flesh. Covered with soft cotton, but still, warm male flesh. A familiar scent flooded her head. A hungry wet heat began to pulse in her womb even before she opened her eyes. *Michael—*

He lay on his side, facing her. Early morning sunlight streamed in through the windows, falling across his face. He had little golden flecks in his blue eyes, Daisy mused. She hadn't noticed that before. His lashes were ridiculously long, especially for a man. He was probably one of the most beautiful men she'd ever seen.

And he was lying in her bed. Daisy swallowed, confused, the cobwebs in her brain keeping her from talking for a minute. Lust and exhaustion did not make it easy to form coherent thoughts. She'd be damned if she'd just babble. Finally, she licked her lips. "I thought you'd left."

"I did." He reached up with his hand, tracing his fingers over her cheek, along her nose and her lips. She shivered under that light touch, but never stopped looking into his eyes.

Damn, he had such beautiful eyes. That dark blue, so warm. Just one look from him was enough to make her get weak in the knees.

He was so big, so full of brutal strength, yet so amazingly gentle. He had cradled Sandy like she was made of glass as he carried her to the car. Sandy had curled up against him, like she knew he would keep her safe. She had good instincts.

"If you left—why are you in my bed?"

A faint smile curled his lips. "Decided to take you up on that offer," he murmured. He moved then, rolling so that she was under him. He settled himself in the cradle of her thighs and she whimpered as hot little jolts of pleasure rocketed through her system.

Daisy would have been really pleased with their positions,

except he was still fully clothed. Licking her lips, she focused on his words and not on how amazing he felt pressed against her. "Offer…"

"Hmmm," he murmured, his voice a low, rough purr as he bent low and pressed his lips against her neck. "The changing my mind thing. You said you wouldn't mind trying to change my mind. I'm here to let you do that. That is, if you can."

For one second, her mind went blank. And then Daisy started to laugh. Wrapping her arms around his neck, she smiled at him, "Oh, yeah. I think I can manage that." Lowering her lashes, she murmured, "And the first order of business is getting you out of those clothes—you have this bad habit of being overdressed…"

He grinned back at her and then all thought fled as he covered her mouth with his.

# SIGN UP FOR SHILOH'S NEWSLETTER

*and be the first to know about new releasees*

# PIECES OF ME

*Now Available*

I woke with a scream echoing in my ears.

It was one a.m. but the lights shone, bright as day, in my room.

Being in the dark was enough to terrify me. Cowering in the middle of my bed, I drew my knees to my chest and shivered.

"I'm free." I drew in a breath, let it out. "I'm free."

The sound of my voice grounded me, a little.

"I'm free."

It took several minutes of breathing, of talking to myself before I no longer felt like the nightmare was going to overwhelm me. Longer still before I was willing to uncurl from the protective ball I'd curled into as the echoes of the dream washed over me.

*I got out,* I told myself. *I got away. He doesn't control me anymore. I'm not just a thing.*

Carefully, feeling like I might break, I got out of bed and padded into bathroom.

"You're you," I said. My voice was rougher than it had once been, husky. A guy at a bar had told me it was sexy as fucking hell—those had been his words.

I wish I could appreciate the compliment. But my sexy as fucking hell voice had happened because I'd spent too much time *trapped* in a very real hell and I'd screamed until I'd damaged my vocal cords.

Hard to appreciate having a phone sex kind of voice when that's what it took to get it.

Still, at least I can talk now. I stared at my pale reflection and spoke again. "You're you. You're Shadow. And you got away."

I was no longer the nothing, the nobody he'd made me. I was no longer just a silent scream in the dark and that was what mattered.

Because the dregs of the dream still clung to me, I stripped out of my clothes and climbed into the shower, turning the water on as hot as I could manage. Standing under the spray until the water started to chill, I let it wash away the stain of the dream as I continued my morning mantra.

*I'm me. I can leave my home. I can go shopping. I can go to the beach.*

"He isn't here to stop me."

Outside, the sun was starting to edge up over the horizon and the fist of terror began to ease. Daytime was always better. I was too old to be afraid of the dark, but I wasn't going to feel shame over that small thing.

I had too many other things to be ashamed of.

Wrapping a towel around myself, I used another to dry my hair and moved to stand in front of the mirror. The woman staring back at me from the mirror looked like an urchin, a wet, bedraggled one.

I turned away from the reflection and grabbed my robe. I'd get coffee. I'd get to work. I'd make myself forget…for a little while.

And I'd pretend it was enough.

It wouldn't be though.

Nothing was ever enough.

There are times in my life when I look back over the years and it's like I'm watching a film of somebody else's life.

My life seemed to stop when I was twenty. Completely stopped, and some other stranger took over. It wouldn't surprise me to see a headstone, complete with my name.

*Here lies Shadow Grace Harper…her life stopped at age 20.*

My name truly is Shadow. My mother loved the TV show ***Dark Shadows***, but the name Barnabas didn't really suit a baby girl and none of the female cast had really appealed. But she liked Shadow Grace and my dad indulged her. Always.

He indulged her, spoiled me. Then, when I was sixteen, they both left me, stolen in a car crash when a tired truck driver fell asleep at the wheel.

I was sent to live with an aunt who barely tolerated my existence.

It wasn't all that terribly bad. I didn't like her, she didn't like me but we managed to co-exist, right up until I turned eighteen. Then I left that tired, gray house behind, heading for the quiet, bucolic charm of Pawley's Island, South Carolina, buying one of the charming old mansions and settling in for what I'd hoped to be the life of an artist.

Life changed a few months later when I realized so many of the kids my age were going off to school. It was too late for me to try to get in anywhere, so I'd spent that year having fun and doing all the things I hadn't been able to do with my aunt, while getting ready to start college a bit later.

At nineteen, I started college—attending the University of Massachusetts. I kept the Pawley's Island house, letting a realtor talk me into using it a vacation property while I was in school, because sooner or later, I'd come back there. I loved Pawley's Island, loved the laziness of the place, loved the sunrises on the beach, the people. Everything about it, really.

But I had college to worry about and my plans had been to pursue…something artsy.

That had been my plan. Something artsy.

At nineteen, with more money than sense, it had been an viable goal in my mind. I'd get a degree and maybe I'd spent my life painting or teaching. Or maybe I'd just find a way to be happy.

Could that be a life's goal? A job? Being *happy*? Finding a way to not be lonely, the way I had been ever since my parents died?

I didn't know. I no longer understood that girl, but then again, that girl died a long time ago.

It was at U-Mass that I met and fell in love a handsome, sophisticated older man. I was twenty when I met Stefan Stockman. He was fifteen years older than me and he was the beginning of the end for the girl I'd been—that silly, foolish Shadow Grace Harper. After a whirlwind courtship that lasted less than six months, we married.

I'd hadn't even turned twenty-one.

We were still on our honeymoon when the change started. It was slow, it was subtle…and it was terrifying. Shadow wasn't a suitable name for his wife, so naturally I became Grace. The loud, boisterous laugh wasn't suitable, so naturally, I learned to laugh quietly, behind my hand…and then I just stopped laughing at all.

Naturally. It all happened naturally.

And naturally, in my mind, it's easier to view it all as something that just happened to somebody else. As a movie. Something that I can view as just somebody's bad dream, not something that happened to me.

The movie ended when I was twenty-five and I woke up in the hospital, just a few short hours after I stumbled out of the basement, freed, oddly enough by a freak tornado that had killed eight people. It killed eight people, but it saved me.

Yet another thing to be ashamed of—the storm killed eight people, shattered the lives of others.

And it freed me. I was so pathetically grateful for it.

Sitting at the table, lost in memories, I sketched, unaware of what I was even drawing until I was done.

When I finished, I found myself staring at a picture of me—my own face. Only it wasn't *right.* My face no longer looked like my own, yet another sign of how completely gone that girl was.

After spending months in hell, after being beaten multiple times, plastic surgery had been required to fix the damage. My cheekbone had been broken and healed badly. Swelling and an infection inside my sinuses had required another surgery, and my nose, also the recipient of several hard blows, needed repair as well.

The last beating had left my jaw fractured jaw and I had scars on my body.

I don't even know where many of the scars came from.

Memories of those months were vague and some were gone completely.

That was another thing I was grateful for—I don't want to remember *any* of that time. Even losing a few memories was blessing.

I looked down at my altered face and the dream came back to me.

I'd tried to leave.

That was what had set him off.

I'd tried to leave and he came after me, dragged me back…and practically threw me away, locking me away someplace so dark, so desolate, nobody had even heard my screams.

The phone rang, making me jump.

"Hello."

"Hello, darling."

I smiled at the sound of the man's voice. Only Seth could call me and immediately make me smile. "You better not flirt with me. Marla will get jealous."

"Marla is standing right here. And she said, *hi, honey.*" Seth imitated his girlfriend's New Jersey accent almost perfectly, drawing another smile from me.

"Tell her I said *hi back*. What are you up to?"

"We're driving up to Myrtle Beach tonight…going to hit a bar or two, get drunk. Ride the Ferris Wheel. Come with."

A pang of longing went through me. "No."

"Come on, babe…come with us. Have fun. We'll go to the beach."

"I can go to the beach here and it's a lot quieter. Also, there was another shark sighting near Myrtle Beach. I don't think so." Sharks weren't what scared me. I'd faced much worse things than sharks. But I wasn't going to tell him that I couldn't handle being in a crowd, unaware of who all was there, who might be watching me.

"If any sharks come near you, I'll chase them off," he promised.

"No, Seth."

He sighed. "Sooner or later, I'm going to get you off Pawley's Island. You need to learn to have fun again, babe."

"I do have fun. Every other Thursday, for movie night."

We chatted for a few more minutes and agreed on a movie for the following day—Thursday, movie night, my favorite day of the week—and then he hung up. After I lowered the phone back to the table, I reached out and traced a finger down the line of my sketched, slightly imperfect jaw.

I wished I had the courage to go with him.

I wished I wasn't so afraid.

But my ex-husband was still out there.

And worse…he knew where I lived.

*****

I sat at the table and looked outside.

When I saw the man sitting on the steps of the house diagonal to mine, I eased back and tried to pretend I hadn't seen him.

He'd seen me, though. I knew he had. After all, he was being paid to sit there and watch and wait. Paid to spy on me.

It was like having my ex-husband there, staring at me, watching me.

A silent reminder, *You'll never be free of me…*

I ran away from him once, but he just found another way to torment me. That fear of him still haunts me, controls me. *He* still haunts me, controls me.

He still watches me and I know it, even though I left Boston and moved back to Pawley's Island. I had money…a lot of it, a fact that probably pissed my ex-husband off. If he could have controlled that money, he could have maybe controlled me, kept me from leaving.

The money was from my parents, a trust fund that had been left for me after their deaths. He was rich himself, but the money I'd inherited once I turned twenty five made his net worth look…paltry. He hadn't realized that I'd only get yearly lump sums until I was twenty five. Then I'd receive the bulk of it.

I'd foolishly let him know about the inheritance that would be mine, but he didn't clue into the deal about the lump sums until later.

If I could figure out how to do it, maybe that money would buy my freedom. Sometimes I fantasized about trying to hire somebody to kill him, but I never followed through.

Other times I thought about buying myself a new life somewhere, a new name.

I had the money.

I'd researched how.

I might even work up the courage to do it.

Nibbling on my thumbnail, I stared around the edge of the curtain at the man paid to spy on me. He sipped his coffee and stared back. It didn't even seem to bother him that he was making my life hell.

Turning my back on him, I shut him out of my mind. At least I tried.

"Find something else to do," I told myself. Find another way to get back at him—not the man on the porch. But *him.* My ex-husband. The man who still sought to control me.

Almost everything I did was some sort of small, subtle rebellion.

Coming back to Pawley's Island, cutting my hair, even the clothes I wore.

I was running out of new ideas, but even walking barefoot to the beach that was just beyond my porch was something that would have had him furious. That was what I would do, I decided. I'd go to the beach.

ঙঙ

I'd pulled on a long flowing skirt and a tank top. Another one of my small rebellions. I looked like a modern day hippy, my short, choppy hair already disheveled from the ever-present breeze. I'd tied a bandana around my wrist. Once I got to work, I'd need it to keep my hair back, but for now, I loved the feel of the wind.

With my bag over my shoulder, I headed out the back door. I don't know how long it would take my shadow to find me. Sooner or later, when I didn't show up through a window, he'd come looking, but for a little while, I was untethered.

There was coffee in a thermos and I munched on toast as I walked. Gulls circled overhead and a few came down to land close by, hoping I'd toss down my meager breakfast. They could hope as much as they wanted. They weren't getting my toast.

My phone beeped just as I reached the table at the very edge of my property, right before it gave way to sand. It wasn't quite ten but others were already hitting the beach and as I pulled out my phone, I studied everybody, distrust as much a part of me as the color of my eyes.

After I'd assured myself that none of them were my ex, I looked at my phone screen. Instinctively, a smile curled my lips.

It was Seth—or rather a picture.

He and Marla were standing by one of the kiosks that rented out movies and he was pretending to gag himself while Marla fanned herself with the chosen movie.

I laughed and texted him back.

*Don't watch it without me.*

The best thing that had happened since I left Boston had been meeting Seth. The hottest, most intense man I'd ever met, when he knocked on my door, he'd terrified me. He'd been with another equally hot man—his lover at the time—and I'd been so scared, I'd barely been able to vocalize two words.

They'd known it, too.

But Seth had refused to leave, insisting that he had something important to tell me. In the end, he'd asked if I could at least meet him at the little coffee shop in town.

I'd agreed.

He'd told me that I had to promise to be there, otherwise, he'd just back and knock—and sing very badly—until I agreed to talk to him.

I'd learned over the years that Seth does sing very badly indeed.

I also learned that his lover Tony would have been just fine if I hadn't met them at the coffee shop.

Seth, though, was a tattooed, tarnished knight, always looking for somebody in distress.

He had a record, petty theft and other issues that had landed him in jail for a year, but he was trying to turn his life around, going to school, paying bills…he explained all of this upfront, while I sat there, confused and not quite following. Then he told me that my ex-husband had approached him.

The pieces clicked and fell together as he explained that my ex had tried to bribe him into watching me.

He lived in the house just across from mine and it would have been a perfect plan, except Seth wasn't an asshole.

My heart had knocked against my ribs the entire time and I'd waited, terrified of what he was going to say, even though a part of me already knew. I'd already seen one of the neighbors who was either really into fruit, or just too fixated on me, because he showed up every time I was at the fruit stand to buy more mangos for the smoothies I'd gotten addicted to.

My ex-husband was having people watch me.

Seth had been willing to testify. We called the cops.

Cops came by to talk to Seth a few days later, then drove off.

When I asked him what happened, he refused to tell me.

But I knew it had something to do with my ex.

I'm surprised he's still my friend.

Tony isn't. They fought for weeks and less than three months after that, Tony moved out.

He met Marla a few months later and they've been together ever since. I think he's seriously in love with her. He had grinned at me when I saw them together and told me, "I never did see the point in tying myself down on anything. I go both ways."

It had made me laugh, even as I wished I could be more like that. I do nothing but tie myself down. To my fear, to the memories. To my husband's controlling nature.

All of it controls me, even now, nearly three years after a storm freed me from hell.

I'd gone back to college, but I never did pursue being an art teacher. That was what I'd wanted…well, before. There was no way I could stand that now. People would watch me. Want to talk to me. Ask me questions.

I went into graphic design instead and that was better. I could work from my home. I was safe there. Safe inside those walls, where he couldn't watch me. Where he couldn't spy.

Where I was alone.

But sometimes…being alone is just too much.

Sometimes, being alone just sucks.

Too often, I still feel like I'm trapped in some awful nightmare.

I'm so desperately ready to wake up.

Sighing, I settled down at my favorite table and took a sip of my coffee. The water was rough today. It matched my mood and I closed my eyes, letting the sound of the waves crashing against the beach sooth me.

*****

The hours passed by too fast, yet it was a slow, almost pleasant crawl. I was blissfully aware of the sun on my back, the wind in my hair.

And him.

There was another reason I loved coming to the beach.

Another reason I liked sitting here.

I don't know his name. He's at the beach almost as often as I am and if he's ever noticed me staring at him, he hasn't given any sign. So I let myself stare and I let myself watch. I let myself wish.

Sometimes, just looking at him makes me hurt inside. It's a pins and needles sort of feeling, like something in me is trying to come back to life, slow, painful life.

I watch him and I think about what it would be like if I had the courage to go up to him and say hi.

If I had the courage.

But he was the kind of man who was forever out of my reach.

It was safer that way, too. He was larger than life, full of heat and energy and a raw kind of masculine beauty that just made the body go almost numb.

He was too intense. Too big. Too there. And he had a way about him that made me think he could be cruel. He had a wolf tattooed across his back and since I didn't know his name, I called him Lobo.

Big, dark and built, he looked like he belonged to the beach. Or maybe the beach belonged to him. His hair was so short, it looked like he buzzed it off with a razor every day he rolled out of bed. Thoughts of him and bed made my heart jump around inside my chest and needs I'd forgotten I even had stirred inside me.

There was a tattoo over his left pectoral, a vivid starburst, although I'd never been close enough to see the details too clearly. On his back was that wolf, a massive, snarling wolf. It started low on his spine, stretched up across the elegant, ridged muscles and finished with the wolf's muzzle around his left shoulder.

Maybe Lobo seemed an odd name for him, but he stalked the beach like a predator and I needed to have some name for him since I couldn't just think *him* every time I saw him, thought of him. Dreamed of him.

And I did dream about Lobo.

The dreams about him were the only respite I had from my nightmares. They were the kind of dreams I hadn't thought I'd ever have again. Sweaty, torrid dreams that had me moaning and clenching my thighs together, longing to touch…and be touched.

Dreams that had me waking feeling empty, filled with longing.

Wishing I was anybody but who I was.

Wishing I had the courage to reach out and take what I wanted, what I needed.

And I so desperately needed.

My skin prickled and I looked up as his gaze casually brushed over me. Our gazes collided and my breath caught in my throat before I looked back down, staring at the sketch in front of me.

It was Lobo again.

He was naked…again.

My favorite way to portray men.

It wasn't always sexual, but lately, that was how I did it. I couldn't find any other means of satisfaction and I didn't see that changing. The fear inside me was too great. It wasn't that I feared sex, exactly. After the first hellish year of my marriage, my husband had stopped wanting sex with me. He used to taunt me with it, because I think he knew I'd wanted it. Not necessarily with him, but…just sex. The connection. The intimacy. The feel of a body pressed against mine. I'd wanted to be wanted. And he'd denied me even that.

Even as he battered me in every other way imaginable. There

were nights when I'd wake up with my face shoved into the pillow while he tore into me and I'd bite my lip blood to keep from crying. When it was over, he'd tell me about the whores, his mistress, even how he had more pleasure just jacking off in the shower—all things that were better at getting him off than me.

And to think I'd thought that was hell. That was nothing. That was easy. I hadn't really known hell until—

My mind shied away. I couldn't think about the final months.

I didn't *want* to, either.

I wanted to think about here…about now.

The beach, the sun shining down on my back, so hot and intense, the wind teasing at my hair, the rhythmic lull of the ocean as the waves crashed into the sand. Voices…always voices. I craved the sound of people now, even if I didn't know them.

Just as I craved the light, the feel of the sun shining down on me, and the sight of people. Old, young, unattractive or so beautiful they made the heart sigh. It didn't matter.

Right now, though, I was sketching the one who made *my* heart sigh and my body yearn.

Sketching out the image of the man. Lobo…the focus of all the hot and crazy dreams. The only focus. The relief from my nightmares.

This sketch was a bad one to be doing here.

He was standing, his back braced against a wooden post, the sand under his feet, waves washing up around him. And his hands were fisted in my hair. I was on my knees in front of him, fully dressed, while I took his cock into my mouth.

Drawing it was the most arousing sort of foreplay, and the most frustrating, because there would be no end, no way to fulfill this aching hunger. Heat gathered in me as I imagined taking that cock inside my mouth, wondering how close I was to *really* capturing how he would look naked. A pulse of hunger throbbed deep inside me and I bit my lip to stifle a groan as I imagined how his hands might tighten to urge me on.

He wouldn't be a gentle lover.

I didn't need a gentle lover, I didn't think.

What I needed, what I *craved*, was a lover, period.

Somebody who wanted me. Needed me.

My face was flushed and hot as I finally finished the sketch. I was going to embarrass myself if I tried another one like that out here. Embarrass myself or just leave myself too shaky to make the walk back home. Unless I took a plunge into the waves crashing against the beach.

I flipped to a fresh sheet of paper and started a new sketch.

His hands this time. Just his hands.

They fascinated me. Long fingers, broad palms.

Were his hands rough? How would they feel rasping—

"Watch out!"

I flinched and cowered, instinctively curling in on myself and not even a second later, pain licked across my cheekbone, spreading up. Numbness hit a second later and that fear, always hidden so close under the surface, crept out.

The football lay on the ground next to me and I stared at it, my eyes tearing as my head started to ache and pound.

The familiar wisp-wisp-wisp of footsteps falling across the sand caught my ears and I jerked my head up, watching as two of the college boys who liked to hang out at the beach came running toward me.

"Hey, are you okay?"

The haze of confusion started to clear and I pieced together what had happened. He wasn't here—my ex. He hadn't found me. Hadn't hit me. I wasn't in danger. It was a football. It had hit me. I was okay. My head hurt and my face hurt, but I was okay. I'd taken so much worse.

"Ma'am?"

The sound of that worried voice almost shattered me and I realized it didn't matter if my ex-husband wasn't here. I was going to fall apart soon.

I jerked my head around and started to gather up my supplies.

Leave. I had to leave.

A hand touched my shoulder and I jerked back, falling on my ass onto the sand.

Now, the slow, hot rush of blood started to creep up my cheeks and those two boys stood over me, watching me. One had a smirk on his face and he didn't bother to hide it. The other looked bewildered. "I just wanted to make sure you're okay," he said, lifting one hand and then letting it fall helplessly to his side. "You…your face is red."

"Leave the freak alone, Tony," his friend said, nudging him in the shoulder. "She looks like she's going to scream rape all because you touched her. Come on, let's—"

The kid turned and stopped in his tracks.

I stopped as well, my breathing frozen, everything in me frozen as horror slammed into me.

He was there, too,. Just a few feet away and he had a grim look on his face.

Lobo. Whatever his name was.

"Ah…hey, Jenks." The long, lanky college kid guy smiled, but even despite my fear, I could see the strain on his face. "How are you?"

Jinx? His name was Jinx? Or maybe it was short…for… for something…Staring at my knees, I tried to get my legs underneath so I could move, get to my feet, get away. But my limbs were frozen. *I* was frozen, all but locked in place with shock and fear and horror. *Get away*. Get *away*.

I tried so hard to deal with the panic attacks. But sometimes, they crept out to bite me in the ass, and this one was so close, I could already feel its teeth.

"How am I?" Lobo asked, his face drawn tight as he took a step toward the kid who'd been mocking me. "You don't want to ask. You pull a shit thing like that and then be an asshole about it? Get the fuck out of here."

As they got out of the fuck out of there, the fear that had frozen me finally loosed its grip and I was able to scramble to my feet and grabbed my things. I had to move. Needed to get out of there. I felt exposed.

So exposed, kneeling on the sand to pick up my sketch pad, the charcoal pencils. The sketch I'd just drawn was right there and I hurriedly snapped the book shut, a blush scalding my cheeks red. I snatched up my pencils, the eraser, everything I'd dropped as fast as I could. As I reached for one of my smaller sketchbooks, a shadow fell across the sand in front of me. A bronzed hand closed around it.

The lump in my throat was going to choke me. I couldn't breathe around it, and I couldn't swallow. But I couldn't stay there, staring at my knees either. Slowly, I dragged my gaze up and met his.

He had pretty eyes, I noticed inanely. Too pretty for that rugged face of his. The dark brown was velvety, almost soft, and spiky, curly lashes framed that velvety brown. Right now, he was watching me with an assessing stare. His gaze roamed over me before shifting to my cheek. Bluntly, he said, "That's going to bruise if you don't ice it."

I don't know why I blurted it out. But the words came rushing up my throat and I couldn't stop them.

"It's not the first time I've been bruised." Absently, I reached up and touched the mark on my face, felt the tenderness of it under my questing fingers. Nothing was broken. Sadly, I knew how that felt, too.

His mouth went tight around the corners and his eyes flattened. He carried a lot of the emotion in his eyes. I couldn't really decipher what those emotions were, but they were there. A straight, thick black brow arched over his eyes. "Yeah? You do anything about it?"

"Not much." I clambered to my feet and shook the sand out of my skirt before I turned back to get the rest of my stuff off the table. "I got away from him. That's about it."

"That's more than most do."

I didn't look at him as I headed off. I didn't run. But it sure as hell felt like it.

# ABOUT THE AUTHOR

J.C. Daniels is the pen name of author Shiloh Walker.
Shiloh Walker has been writing since she was a kid. She fell in love with vampires with the book Bunnicula and has worked her way up to the more…ah…serious works of fiction. She loves reading and writing anything paranormal, anything fantasy, and nearly every kind of romance. Once upon a time she worked as a nurse, but now she writes full time and lives with her family in the Midwest. She writes romantic suspense and contemporary romance, and urban fantasy as J.C. Daniels.

Learn more about J.C. at www.jcdanielsblog.com

Sign up for her newsletter at shilohwalker.com and have a chance to win a monthly giveaway.

Twitter: @shilohwalker
FB: https://www.facebook.com/AuthorShilohWalker